ROBERT STEWARD was born in London in 1943 and is an honours graduate of the University of Surrey. His lifetime career as a professional engineer in the electronics industry enabled him to contribute to development projects that in their turn launched products that are readily recognisable as commonplace in contemporary society. In support of this work his authorship has produced copious amounts of technical reports and documentation. He lives on the south coast of Hampshire with his wife and youngest son at home. His other three sons live independently in the area.

GW00726004

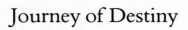

Journey of Destiny

Journey of Destiny

Robert Steward

ATHENA PRESS
LONDON

First Published 2006 by
ATHENA PRESS
Queen's House, 2 Holly Road
Twickenham TW1 4EG
United Kingdom

Printed for Athena Press

To Eileen and for Cornwall

Chapter One

Robert had a particularly arduous final year at Imperial College. The final year's syllabus had just about finished him. The science with mathematics had grown particularly hard and his expectation for an excellent final result had diminished.

The worst aspect was the last Easter holiday break, where he had elected to spend the period in college residence in order to revise completely for the final exams with minimum distraction. The hall was deserted and no catering was available. One or two of his fellow undergraduate friends were there, and there was great relief to be had in their company after the self-imposed study periods. Rise latish, study most of the morning, out for lunch with friends to the nearest transport café, where they did a tolerable steak pie and chips for 1s 10d. Back to the hall for afternoon study, heavens only knew how tea was conjured up and then on to evening study, looking forward to the late meeting up with the friends for coffee, cards, cigarettes and as much humour as could be endured. Finally then to crash into bed, with a sigh of relief, temporarily relieved from the agony of study till morning!

The worst aspect was over; the final exams were taken and hope for some sort of second was there, that would enable the possibility of decently salaried employment. The post-study and post-exam delirium was endured in different ways. One friend took to a hot bath, nursing a bottle of Scotch; others went for the inevitable booze-up. Robert and his friends visited a traditional riverside pub, drank copiously of the local ale and sang lustily the traditionally ribald rugby songs.

On another day, a visit to an out-of the-suburbs pay-as-you-go golf course was taken with a relaxing clubhouse lunch. The round was terrible in terms of score but wonderful in terms of countryside for one cooped up for so long in a studious environment in the midst of a busy city.

Well, that was all behind him now and as the taxi drew into Paddington Station, he relished with anticipation the journey on the 9 a.m. Cornish Riviera Express to the West Country, to join his Cornish relatives for an extended stay. These train journeys had always been thrilling for him, from early childhood. His parents lived in a very neat north-west London suburb. London was the town of his birth, but the lure of Cornwall was always present, imbued in him by his Cornish mother's repeated tales of her life there.

The carriage and compartment were found easily, and the luggage was loaded in the overhead rack. Thankfully, the compartment was empty apart from him and he settled in and made himself comfortable. Plenty of room to stretch out in! Restlessness compelled him to go to the window. He pulled the leather strap to raise and then drop the window, securing it about halfway down by means of the strap; fastening it onto the brass door stud. He looked out towards the engine and the old familiar scene was there. Half the carriages of the train stretched before him and the engine stood sentinel at the head. The familiar smell of smoke and steam came back to him, and the awesome power of the engine was only too evident from the shocking blasts issuing from it, even whilst stationary. He made a mental note to remember not to lean out of the window when the train was travelling at full speed, as painful memories of cinders catching him in the eye from the smoke stream were still with him.

Relaxing back into his seat, he observed the compartment and was pleased to see the sepia photographic pictures of pleasant holiday resorts displayed just above the headrests covered with the clean white napkins. Reassured, he leant his head back and rested it on a clean napkin and was beginning to unwind fully for the first time since those trying final exams. He stretched back and reached into the deep pocket of his sports jacket and pulled out a packet of twenty Players medium and a box of Swan Vestas. He tapped one end of the cigarette on the packet, inserted it between his lips and lit it with a red-topped match. He took a long draw. That sense of all-pervading calm came upon him, fuelled by the effect of the nicotine now coursing through his blood-stream and having that narcotic effect on his brain's sense of well-being.

All was well. Just wait for the train to pull out and for a relaxing, scenic journey.

The shrill shriek of the stations guard's whistle blew in unison with the increasing steam blast from the engine. The train was just ready to pull out for the journey. Simultaneously, Robert's tranquillity in the compartment was interrupted with a sudden crashing back of the compartment door and the breathless entry of a person into the compartment, accompanied by a porter struggling with heavy luggage.

'You just made it ma'am. Just in time.'

'Yes, just in time,' replied a female voice. 'Thank you very much for your help.'

The porter laboured to lift the two pieces of luggage hastily into the rack. The lady thanked him again, gave him a tip and the porter was gone, alighting rapidly from the carriage as the train began to pull out of the station.

Robert's peace now disturbed, he looked up and regarded the fellow occupant of the compartment, who by now had settled herself into the diagonally opposite corner of the compartment, next to the corridor and facing away from the engine. Robert was facing the engine, the position he always preferred on a long journey.

He glanced across at her and saw an attractive young woman in a flowery summer dress, with a small, lightweight jacket draped across her shoulders. She had the look of an 'out-of-town' girl with a pleasant face. She caught his glance and smiled, and Robert was obliged to return the smile.

'Just managed to catch the train,' she blurted out, 'just as well, otherwise I would have had to wait until tomorrow for the next one!'

'Oh, that's good then, you would not have wanted to wait another day to catch the train you want, would you? It was worth the rush,' said Robert clumsily.

Both fell silent after the exhaustion of that initial flurry of conversation.

Robert was relaxed though tired, and he knew himself that he was not a great conversationalist with young women, finding it rather difficult to make headway with them at times. They often had ideas with which he could not find mutual accord. He was somewhat captive to his scientific, mathematical background, which always made it difficult for him to make general, chatty conversation, particularly the conversation that might interest a young woman. Too long at the study grindstone, he was afraid, but there was always hope! He glimpsed across again, endeavouring to restart the conversation with her, and then noticed that she had already started reading a magazine which she had pulled out of her handbag, and seemed fairly absorbed in it. Ah well, he thought, I'll rest easy. Maybe she is getting out after a few stops anyway, and it is hard going chatting!

The journey was well under way; the train had left the environs of London and was steaming at top speed through the most scenic countryside. Robert settled back into his seat, lulled into drowsiness by the rhythmic clickety-click of the train carriage wheels crossing the rail gaps. He glanced casually out of the window at the passing scenery and thought to himself, how pleasant to observe such beautiful countryside for such little effort.

He reached into his pocket for another Players cigarette and before lighting it, looked across to the girl to confirm her agreement to his smoking, but she was deeply engrossed in the magazine. He lit up anyway, and puffed the smoke towards the vent of the open window. He enjoyed his cigarettes. He enjoyed their stimulus; they had helped him enormously to concentrate during his studies and were excellent for calming anxiety, but he was well aware that they were killing his chest. I may have to stop one day, but for the moment I'll continue enjoying them, he reassured himself.

The white-jacketed, green-cuffed, well-turned-out steward drew back the compartment's sliding door with a well-practised flourish that ended in a distinct thud, designed no doubt to wake up dozing passengers. 'Coffee! Coffee! Morning coffee, would sir and madam like morning coffee?' The coffee trolley was not yet in evidence but the steward was taking orders.'

Robert looked up and said, 'Yes, a morning coffee would be most welcome.'

The girl in turn looked up, but seemed hesitant in making up her mind. Robert invited, 'join me in one.'

'Oh, all right then, but not particularly strong, please.' The trolley arrived and a second steward began pouring. He braced himself in the doorway against the motion and jolts of the train and poured with the consummate ease of one well versed in the skill. The milk and sugar were proportioned according to taste and Robert pressed a two-shilling piece into his hand accompanied by a three penny bit as a tip.

'Thank you very much, sir!' was the response and, 'Lunch is served from 12 until 1.30 p.m. in the dining car.'

'Thank you,' said Robert. The steward slid the compartment door shut with a gentler movement than he had used to open it, and moved on. Robert sipped his coffee and relished the taste. He looked across at the girl and said, 'Coffee all right?'

'Yes, thank you very much, just to my taste – not too strong.'

Robert continued, 'First stop Exeter I believe, quite some time yet though.'

'Yes, well after midday,' she replied. 'I have been up and down on this line many times and Exeter is always a long time off from Paddington.'

Robert's curiosity was aroused. 'Oh, you use this line often do you?'

'Yes, I have some occasional business to attend to in London, and whilst there I stay with relatives for two or three days. It's too long a journey to return the very next day.'

Robert replied, 'Well, I've used this line quite a bit over the years. Cornish relatives, you know. Often go and stay with them. In fact, I'm staying with an aunt in Bodmin for a few weeks this time for a bit of rest and relaxation.'

'You need rest and relaxation?' she replied curiously.

'Yes, I've been studying hard and need a good break before taking up some full-time employment.' He then went on to explain that he had studied science and mathematics, and that he hoped for a good career in that line.

'You must be very clever to understand all that,' she said.

'Not particularly,' he replied, 'just hard work and application.'

Eager to get off the treadmill of actually having to explain tricky subjects, he said, 'and what about you?'

She reddened up a little, suddenly becoming the centre of

attention. 'I live with my parents at the moment, and I housekeep for my mother and brothers. My father and brothers farm on Bodmin moor; mainly dairy but with some arable. I did go to agricultural college, but could not keep it up as help was needed at home and on the farm, and for some other reasons…' She trailed off.

Robert burst in enthusiastically, 'Bodmin moor,' he exclaimed, 'right next to where I'll be staying. It's excellent there, very atmospheric, but can be very wet as all British moors are. I expect then that you will be getting out at Bodmin Road Station?'

'Yes,' she replied, 'my parents are meeting me there with the car. It's difficult to get back to the farm without a car. Very few buses.'

'My aunt will be meeting me too at the station with her car, it's even difficult to get into Bodmin from there as well.'

'Your aunt drives?' she said.

'Yes,' he replied, 'a very independent widowed lady, she has to, to get around.'

'That's very good,' she said, 'not too many women drivers around.'

'Well then, we are both on this train for the duration, we'll arrive at Bodmin Road together!' She smiled in reply. Robert noticed that her looks were enhanced with this smile, and his interest in her grew. Thoughts of even seeing her occasionally whilst he was down there began to course through his head. That could make a nice change rather than kicking around alone, as was so often the case when he was away. Female company in the same age group would make a pleasant change.

The train thundered on, under bridges, past signal boxes, through tunnels on its iron road, creating that rhythmic motion, straining to fulfil its designer's specification to reach its destination in record time.

Robert glanced at his watch. It was 12.30 already. Time had flown since the beginning of the journey. A steward looked in through the door. 'Second sitting for lunch now, please, second sitting for lunch,' and then moved, on repeating his call, until it was lost under the engine noise level.

Yes I do feel somewhat peckish by now. It was an early start and I had no breakfast in the rush to catch the train, thought

Robert. I'll treat myself to a decent lunch rather than the transport café style for a change. I do have sufficient finances, after all, the legacy from my good old uncle is still holding out in spite of the ravages of tuition fees, college dinners and some drinking, he mused to himself.

'Would you care to join me for lunch?' he spoke out to the girl. 'I am a bit peckish by now and I really feel in need of recharging my energy.'

'I don't know,' said the girl, 'it's a bit expensive, isn't it, and I have brought a few sandwiches.'

'Have them for tea,' said Robert, 'I can manage the finances and it's best not to eat alone.'

'Are you sure you can afford it?' she replied.

'Yes,' he responded 'I'm not too badly off at the moment and it will be a pleasure to lunch with you.'

Refusal would have been impossible after this and she responded, 'Yes, I would love to, thank you.'

They made their way to the dining car. Robert was leading. It was at least five carriages on. They always seemed to be a heck of a distance away from where you were sitting, thought Robert, swaying with the motion of the train as they negotiated their way through the somewhat fragile-looking carriage junctions with their concertina fabric wall coverings. Passing other passengers in the corridors was always difficult to negotiate. One flattened oneself against the carriage wall and the other person squeezed past, or vice versa.

Robert was conscious of her following him, but they did not speak on the way. After what seemed like a long struggle to get there, they arrived. The dining car steward greeted them with, 'Table for two, sir?' and conducted them to a table that was spare at the other end of the car. They were seated, and menus were placed in their hands.

The lunch for the day seemed quite reasonable. A starter of melon with ginger, followed by a choice of Dover Sole, Hereford Lamb Chop or Home Counties Roast Beef, and a choice of pudding to follow.

Robert chose the Dover Sole, as he was keen on fish, and she chose the Hereford Lamb Chop.

They sat facing one another across the table both realising that this was the first time they had both seen one another face to face. Robert realised that he did not know her name and, for that matter, nor did she know his.

'I'm Robert by the way, Robert Brett.' He held out his hand towards her, 'pleased to meet you.'

She took his hand briefly and responded with 'I'm Juliet, Juliet Mentreath, very pleased to meet you, Robert.'

Lunch proceeded very amicably. It was a good meal. Robert washed his down with a couple of glasses of white wine, and Juliet had a small orange juice. Coffee was served at the end and they continued talking at great length on their respective families. Juliet talked on farming and its difficulties, and on her parents and brothers. Robert talked on his interest in science and possible future work, and on his parents but not on brothers or sisters, being an only child. His father's wartime RAF service was mentioned, and Juliet's father endeavouring to feed the local population under wartime restrictions.

Robert warmed to her and the discernible Cornish burr in her accent. She seemed to warm towards him as well and to like his reasonably intelligent, cultured manner. They observed one another's faces across the table and both liked what they saw, although they both had a natural reticence about them and certainly were not too forward.

'Excuse me, sir,' boomed the voice of the steward, 'I have to ask you to leave the dining car now. We are nearly at Exeter, and we lose the dining car there.'

'Of course,' said Robert, hurriedly paying the bill. It was 10s 6d. Not too bad, he thought, particularly including wine! He tipped the waiter a shilling and they departed quickly to re-enter their carriage and compartment.

The train screeched into Exeter Station before they got back to their compartment. Robert could see some new passengers getting into the train and his thoughts as a consequence were, would they still have the compartment to themselves?

Alas no, a family was already seated. A mother and father and two children. Because of this, Robert and Juliet were obliged to be reseated but as luck would have it they were reseated side by side, facing the engine, by the window. The stop was very short at Exeter and the train was soon on its way towards Plymouth, the next stop before crossing Saltash Bridge, Isambard Brunel's famous construction.

The family was not a particular bother; the children were well behaved and were absorbed in reading through a stack of comic books. Ideal for a rail journey! A few polite asides were made with the mother and father on holidays and the weather, but the interest in pursuing further subjects soon waned.

Robert and Juliet sat side by side, intensely aware of one another's presence and continued with the conversation where they had left off from lunch. Facts on their lifestyles and interests were shared, and they discovered they had much in common. Robert thought, She is very compatible with me and I feel comfortable with her. I would welcome her company in my pursuits. He sensed that she felt the same with him.

The train was coming to that most interesting stretch of line after leaving Exeter at about 1.30 p.m., through the long dark tunnel and then bursting out on the bank of the Exe (an estuary of considerable size). The train's speed was reduced somewhat and the train hurtled over the sharp curves round the coast between Dawlish and Teignmouth. It seemed impossible to have a railway line so close to the sea, you were almost in it. Sea spray could reach the engine, how thrilling! Juliet sensed Robert's inward thrill in this magnificent section of run.

'Never fails to impress, no matter how many times you have been on this run, does it?' She looked into Robert's face for an acknowledgement.

Slightly embarrassed, he made a small smile back at her but said nothing. She understood that he found this moment magical and timeless and it was better to experience it without trying to explain it with less than adequate words. The engine then picked up speed, steaming on to Newton Abbot.

Robert slumped back into his seat, reaching in to his pocket for the Players. 'Good Lord, after all that excitement, I need a cigarette,' he exclaimed. He proffered one to Juliet despite knowing that ladies generally never smoked, and if they did it was never in public. It seemed polite to do so.

'Heavens, no thank you,' she said, as though she found the thought rather shocking. But to placate him she said, 'my father and brothers do, more pipes than cigarettes. Sometimes the farm kitchen gets in quite a fug. My mother hates it, but I do quite like the smell of my father's pipe tobacco. I find cigarette smoke a little bit acrid though. But please do carry on yourself – we are in a smoking compartment and the window is open!'

Robert, taking the permission to carry on, lit up and inhaled deeply, but was careful to direct the exhaled smoke towards the open window.

He coughed. 'Must give up one day, this will be the death of me!' Juliet made no comment on this remark.

The train thundered on. Smoke and steam was streaming back past the window, and the smell of engine smoke was beginning to enter the compartment. 'I'll close the window, shall I?' Robert said, addressing the compartment. They nodded in assent and he got up and released the leather catch from the brass securing stud. He pulled up on the strap and the window thudded and closed. He secured the strap and sat down.

Turning to Juliet, he said, 'We should reach Plymouth around 4 p.m. and then Bodmin Road by about 4.30 p.m. We don't stop for long at Plymouth.'

'Sometimes the navy loads up equipment at Plymouth, bound for Culdrose and that causes delay,' she responded.

'Ah well,' said Robert, 'that should be interesting!'

The train slowed; they were approaching Plymouth. It hissed and screeched and slowed to a halt at the station. The engine hissed, otherwise it was very quiet. The sky was grey and overcast, and typical West Country weather – fine rain – seemed to be gathering. Bang, bang, bang – the freight compartment doors were being opened and closed, and true to Juliet's prediction, sailors were seen loading up wooden-boxed items. This took about a quarter of an hour before the train pulled slowly out of the station and slowly across Isambard Brunel's bridge. The bridge spanned the Tamar, that notable stretch of river separating Cornwall from Devon and from the rest of England.

Robert said, 'We must see this,' and jumped up to stand in the corridor. Juliet joined him, as did the children from the compartment. They were getting excited about crossing the bridge too! Robert and Juliet leaned against the corridor window rail and looked down to the water as the train rolled slowly over the bridge.

It was a magnificent iron bridge – built all those years ago and still standing. Attractive too, its design was well ahead of its time, thanks to the genius of Brunel. Modern constructions of a similar nature were never quite so attractive.

The train continued slowly over the bridge and past the creeks where the old warships were laid up. Battleships, still with fifteen-inch guns, but awaiting the scrapyard. What an ignominious end for such magnificent ships. Juliet sensed his mood – yes, it was a great shame that they had to be scrapped. The modern navy was thinning down and taking a new shape for the new post-war age.

The children lost interest and returned to the compartment. The door slid shut. Robert and Juliet remained standing at the corridor rail looking down to the creeks and countryside. It seemed that they were the only people in the world with such a mutual interest.

Not too long now to Bodmin Road. The train snaked into the forested area surrounding Bodmin Road Station. The rain was fairly streaming down by now, casting an air of quiet gloom. Robert's heart was thumping. I really must arrange to meet her whilst I am down here and not mess it up as so often has happened in the past, he thought.

'Juliet whilst I'm down staying with my aunt I would very much like to meet with you again,' he blurted out.

'Yes, I would like that too,' she responded, a little hesitantly. 'I'll give you the address of the farm. It's not much use giving the telephone number at the moment, as most of the lines on the moor are down due to the post office changing everything over to the new STD telephone network.'

The train drew slowly into Bodmin Road station and there was a surprisingly large crowd waiting, with umbrellas up and wearing raincoats. That's unusual, thought Robert, as generally Bodmin Road was pretty deserted. Like those out-of-the-way stations in those western films. Well, it is holiday time and lots of relatives must be being picked up at this time, he mused.

They both craned their necks, looking for their respective relatives through the open window, but it was impossible to see people with all the umbrellas up and with the rain masking the view. The train ground to a halt and the deep silence descended that one could only find in a Cornish country station, broken only by the hiss of engine steam.

Robert helped Juliet on to the platform with her luggage, and returned to the compartment for his own. His was lighter than hers and he had less trouble carrying it.

He descended from the train again, but there was no sign of Juliet. She is probably waiting at the barrier, he thought, I'll find her there. He walked to the barrier, braving the rain, and heard, 'Robert, Robert dear!' It was his aunt, looking just the same as ever. Straw hat, glasses, tweed suit and pearls, all covered with a see-through plastic mac. She limped slightly with her built-up shoe. 'Lovely to see you my dear, did you have a good journey?' she said.

'Fine, Aunt Hild, thank you, you look so well.' Robert had always used that diminutive for Hilda from his childhood. They embraced.

They walked to the ticket barrier exchanging small talk, and Robert looked out for Juliet. She was nowhere to be seen. She must be outside, he thought. They went to his aunt's car in the station yard (a black Austin with running boards and one wind-screen wiper and lever indicators) and he loaded up his luggage.

'Well, my dear,' said his aunt 'back to Bodmin town for a nice hot pasty and tea, and to get out of this rain!'

Robert normally would have thought nothing could be better, but at the moment he was desperate for a sight of Juliet. 'Just a moment, Aunt, please, I must have a look for a person I was talking to on the train.'

'That's all right my dear, I'll wait in the car.'

He ran into the station yard and observed everybody. He looked into every car leaving. His heart was pounding. No sight of her whatsoever. People were leaving and he could not see her. Finally, everybody had left and he had not seen her! Why did this happen? he thought. Was she whisked away rapidly in her father's car? He had not even got the address he was offered. What was the reason for her disappearing like that? Where had she gone? He walked back, crestfallen, to his aunt's car, thinking, How stupid that this should have happened. I should have stuck to her like glue.

Unlike other failed encounters he could not dismiss this one so easily. He felt desperate to meet her again. The only hope I have is the fact that she lives out on the moor and can't be too far away. I'll have to trace her. Damn, he thought, how stupid, I'm sure she did not deliberately run out on me. I'm sure that there must be a reasonable explanation for this foul-up.

He got into his aunt's car. 'Did you find him?' she said.

'No, she must have been picked up and driven away swiftly – probably due to the wet weather.' He really wanted a cigarette, but he knew that his aunt didn't like him smoking in the car, so he resigned himself to not having one.

'Off to Bodmint,' she said. She often used that little colloquialism for the town. It was a family joke.

'Off to Bodmint then, Aunt,' he said and slumped back into the leather seat. Unbeknown to his aunt, his head was whirling with thoughts of Juliet. How would he ever locate her again?

His aunt clonked the long gearstick into first and the car pulled out of the station yard, on the way to Bodmin.

Chapter Two

Robert awoke. He was still very sleepy and had difficulty adjusting to the realisation of where he was. Oh, I am at my aunt's in Bodmin, how wonderful, and he fell back and luxuriated in the comforting thought of it all. How lovely to be here again. He anticipated with relish the things that lay in store for him in this fine house and good town. Sufficient light was filtering through the heavy brocade curtains for him to glance at his watch on the bedside table to see the hands at 7.20 a.m. Robert did wake early but often went back to sleep again until much later. College life had altered his body clock and he would have to adjust to normal business hours eventually, but not just yet! The house was very quiet. No sound of his aunt moving about just yet.

Robert peered through the gloom and around the room. He could just discern the artefacts in the room. The Victorian dresser was there with the small rectangular mirror on top, between the silver-backed hairbrushes on a silver tray and the gentleman's shaving accoutrements housed in their leather case. The wash-stand cabinet came next into view, with a large, ornate jug and bowl sitting on the marble top. Towels were hanging from a rail at the end of the stand. The tall, heavily embossed wardrobe was at the far end of the room, next to the Hepplewhite chest of drawers. The old prints of the 'Rake's Progress' by Hogarth were still there, surmounted by a plain cross.

Nothing had changed. Robert knew that the washstand was now superseded by the bathroom just along the landing, which gave its cold and hot water via a very old geyser. Occasionally the geyser did not work and hot water for shaving and other uses was carried in boiled kettles from the kitchen to the bathroom. The bath stood on its large feet, huge and made of white enamelled iron. It was also fed from the geyser but took an eternity to fill. The deceased uncle's razor strop hung in its position next to the large washbasin as always. Robert knew that he did not have to hurry out of bed just yet and drifted back into a slumber.

He was roused from his sleep by a knocking at the door. 'Come in, come in,' he mumbled as he struggled to wake himself from that deeper slumber he had fallen into. The door opened and Hilda walked in, carrying a tea tray with biscuits which she carefully settled on the bedside table.

'Hello dear, have you slept well?' she said.

'Yes, thank you, Aunt,' said Robert sleepily.

'Breakfast will be ready for you when you come down, but no hurry just yet. I know you are tired, so rest on for a while.' Hilda walked to the door with her characteristic limp. Robert looked at her. She was attired in a silken dressing gown and her hair, usually in a plaited bun, hung streaming down her back, almost fully grey, but with some darker streaks still present. Her complexion was rosy and healthy. For her years, thought Robert, she is remarkably youthful, and so hospitable. Long may she remain so, he thought. She loved company particularly now since she was widowed.

Robert lifted himself on his elbow and turned his attention to the tea and biscuits. He loved that tray, with the beads threaded on a rod around the edge. It had fascinated him since childhood, when he always twirled the beads! The tea was piping hot and in a white porcelain cup. Good, he thought, Rich Tea biscuits. He broke one with a satisfying snap, bit off a portion, dunked the rest and washed it down with the good, strong tea. The Cornish always made strong, sugary tea or 'ta' as it was pronounced but Robert took his without sugar. His mother used to make it very sweet, but with much effort Robert had eventually persuaded her not to sugar it for him.

Robert had drunk his tea when the loss of Juliet suddenly came upon him very heavily. The events of yesterday evening had somewhat mollified this, however, the thoughts of losing her at this moment began to cause him anguish. Would he find her again? His aunt had driven him into the environs of Bodmin, past Priory Park, past the parish church of St Petroc's, turning into Castle Hill a short way up and then left into Miss Mudge's farmyard. Aunt Hilda had an arrangement with Miss Mudge to garage her car in one of the disused barns. The steepness of Castle

Hill did not allow for any parking on the road and the period of the houses had not taken into account the possibility of twentieth-century car parking! They had walked across the road to the house. It stood there in its late Georgian splendour. An inviting central door with a long sash window either side and three above. Three interestingly-furnished bedrooms, one old bathroom, separate 'throne room', huge kitchen, pantry, cellar, comfortable lounge and regal dining room. The carefully-tended front garden led to a granite-stepped portico, via a sloping-up hard path The neighbouring two houses formed a neat bow with it and St Petroc's church tower was silhouetted in the background, awaiting the tolling of the 'evening curfew' bell at 8 p.m.

The entrance hall greeted them with its vivid row of de'Condamy hunting prints: the Meet, the Gallop, the Chase and the Finish. The hat stand held its array of walking sticks, shooting sticks, fishing rods and wet weather clothing, positively inviting one to participate in outdoor activity and country sport. They went through the inner door in the hall, its coloured glass panel casting blue and red streaks along the hall from the evening sun. Hilda went into the kitchen and Robert took his luggage up to his room.

After depositing his cases in his room, Robert joined his aunt at the large square table in the kitchen for a hot cup of tea and a delicious pasty with tomato chutney. The ensuing conversation was full of catching up on his parents, the aunts, uncles and cousins, and, as the evening drew on, his aunt saw that he was looking increasingly tired and said, 'get thee to bed now, there will be plenty more catching up to do tomorrow. I'll finish up down here.' She often spoke in an old English vein, inculcated from much exposure to the King James version of the Bible.

Gratefully Robert conceded, and pulled himself up the stairway with the aid of the curving banister. A quick splash in the bathroom, teeth, and then to bed. Oh Juliet, he thought, where did you get to? Then he fell asleep.

Oh well, I'd better rouse myself and go down to breakfast, he thought, back in the present. He staggered to the bathroom. He was not a morning person! Shaved and washed, he returned to his room. He dressed casually for the morning. Corduroy trousers, polo-necked sweater and suede shoes. He walked down the staircase, running his hand over the banister. He had often slid down there as a lad, but now dared not. He entered the kitchen and found his aunt in full array. The frying pan was smoking heavily and the preferred countryman's breakfast of bacon, eggs, hogs pudding and fried bread, was well advanced.

'Sit yourself down my dear, Auntie will soon have it ready for you.'

Whilst Robert sat at the huge kitchen table and waited, he reacquainted himself with the kitchen. The large dresser was full with china, willow pattern pottery and engraved glasses. He particularly liked the 'Angler's prayer', hung over the fireplace mantelpiece. It was burnt on to a wooden plaque: 'Oh Lord, give me grace to catch a fish so big that even I when speaking of it afterwards may never need to lie.' Aunt Hilda had been a great fisherwoman in her day along with her husband, with whom she had pursued all manner of country sports. She had taught Robert, when young, to fish for the brown trout, so prolific in the local streams and rivers, and he was still partial to fishing. The motto on the milk jug at the centre of the table always intrigued him. 'Life is chiefly froth and bubble, two things stand as stone, kindness in another's trouble, courage in your own.' The motto on the sugar bowl always amused him. 'Take one, not the lot!'

His aunt placed the huge cooked breakfast before him, and poured him a cup of tea. 'Eat up my dear, it will do you good. I thought that you were looking a bit thin – it must be all those poor meals at college.'

Well, yes, thought Robert, but they weren't that bad! He thanked her and their conversation continued on the theme of last night and what had been happening in Bodmin, with the neighbours and friends, and in the local farming community.

Robert ate with relish, finding that the hogs pudding was delicious. You did not get this in London very often, if at all, he thought. Toast and marmalade followed, with more cups of tea. His aunt only had toast and marmalade, but was always pleased to cook for guests. She presided over them with much pleasure and one really wanted for nothing.

A movement outside the kitchen window distracted them. 'Oh, it's only Miss Mudge,' said Aunt Hilda, 'going up with her cows.' She chuckled. 'She's like a hen fore day, never on time.'

It was well past 10.30 a.m. Any sensible farmer would have had his cattle in the fields at the crack of dawn, and back in the early afternoon for milking. Not Miss Mudge – she always took them late and returned them late. Heavens knows when she did the milking. Her churns, never very many, were always a day behind, waiting at the gate. She styled herself a lady farmer and performed the tasks of farming at her leisure! Robert knew this well, as he had observed this ritual either in the morning or evening over many years from his childhood days of staying with his aunt.

'Go and look, Robert,' she said, 'there she is.'

Robert went to the window and saw her leisurely driving her cows up the hill to the fields above. Why the fields were so distant from the farm one did not know, but one could surmise that the town had grown around the farm and the fields had been 'pushed' further away. Robert looked out and there she was. Brown coat, stick in hand and the same old hat on her head. She must have had it for years. It was rather like a trilby with the brim pulled down, and the hatband was green with verdigris. She looked older, her hair was streaked with grey and on her face, the jowls hung down and she was almost beginning to resemble her cows. A touch of sympathy and admiration flickered through Robert's mind. She is getting old, she never married and is rather eccentric, looks after her old housebound mother, but she keeps going. How did she get into this state? I suppose she will fade out in time, though she is certainly a character to be treasured, he thought.

'She is still going strong then, Aunt,' said Robert.

''Ess, she is, my dear,' said his aunt, reverting to the Cornish abbreviation for yes. 'She will carry on so.'

'It's good to see her again,' he said, and moved back to the table and sat down.

'Aunt,' said Robert, 'I am very pleased to be down staying with you again, but I must admit I am a trifle distressed at the moment.'

'Why, my dear whatever is the matter?' responded Hilda, very concerned.

'Well,' continued Robert, 'you know when you picked me up at the station yesterday evening…'

'I know how tired you were looking,' she interjected.

'Yes, Aunt, but remember I told you I had met someone on the train who had disappeared at the station. Well, that person was a young woman. We were both getting along famously together and I feel quite distressed that after hoping to meet her again, she went off from the station so rapidly that I did not get a chance to make an arrangement.'

Hilda thought for a moment, sensing a romantic connection. 'Well, if she got off at Bodmin Road, she must live around here somewhere,' she said.

'Yes, precisely,' responded Robert. 'She did say she lived out on the moor, and was from a farming family.'

'That narrows it down a bit,' said Hilda. 'I know farmers out on the moor!'

Robert recollected that she did.

'Did you get her name?'

'Yes,' he said, 'Juliet.'

'Hmm…I don't recall hearing a Juliet spoken of out there,' said Hilda. 'Did she not give another name, a surname perhaps?'

Robert thought for a moment – yes, yes she did, but as much as he thought, he could not recollect it. He racked his brains but his mind drew a blank. 'I just cannot think of it, I just cannot remember what it was,' he said frantically.

'Don't distress yourself, my dear, have another cup of tea. Calm down and I'm sure it will come to you 'fore too long,' she said.

The church clock struck eleven o'clock. 'Is that the time? Must be getting along,' said Hilda.

'Do you want a hand with anything?' asked Robert.

'No, that's all right, my dear,' said the independently-minded Hilda, 'you go and relax in the lounge, I'll deal with this.' She meant the washing-up. She did not want men-folk interfering where they shouldn't. Women had their domain and men theirs, and men's was certainly not in the kitchen! She was quite content to organise and run her household herself and did not want any 'interfering' as she put it. Even when her sister Winnie, Robert's mother, stayed, there were well-controlled hackles raised about who ran the kitchen!

Robert walked to the lounge. Two chintz-covered comfortable armchairs were either side of the fireplace. The grate was open with the poker lying across it on some ashes. Being late summer, the evenings were beginning to cool down so his aunt had presumably already lit a fire in there. The highly-polished brass fender surrounded the tiled hearth in which sat the coal-scuttle. The mantelpiece had various old pottery ornaments on it, bracketed at either end by a china bookend dog. Robert slumped into the armchair furthest from the window and was pleased to see the tall cigarette ashtray with the silver matchbox case attached standing in the hearth. Aunt did not mind smoking in the house as long as it was confined to one room, the lounge. After all, the menfolk had to smoke somewhere! He lit up a Players, inhaled, relaxed back into the chair and surveyed the rest of the room. The prayer chair was still there over by the window. A low seat, with a high sloping back and a rolled top. Ideal for kneeling on the seat, leaning against the back, resting your elbows on the rolled top and saying your prayers! He wondered whether it was ever used extensively in its day or whether it was just a fad at the time.

A Louis XVI cabinet was against the wall facing the window. Japanned black with heavily embossed gold tracery and bosses. Very impressive. Above was a black and white print of the ruined Pont d'Avignon. A very pastoral scene. Nothing quite like a romantic ruin for arousing interest in an age gone by! Against the wall adjacent to the door was a slenderly built china cabinet, containing a lifetime's collection of ceramic ornaments and formal chinaware.

Robert looked out of the window across the front garden and to the church tower. He could just pick out the clock face from this distance, and the hands were moving up towards twelve o'clock. The quarter to the hour struck, and Robert inhaled again from his cigarette and blew the smoke out to the centre of the room. What was Juliet's surname? he pondered. He picked up the *Western Morning News* and idly scanned through without being captivated by any particular news item until his eye fell on the classifieds section and his attention was drawn to a particularly large advert for 'Mentreath's Provender. Best Feed in the West. St Austell.'

'Yes,' he exclaimed, 'that was it!' That was Juliet's surname – 'Mentreath'. He jumped up and rapidly hurried to his aunt in the kitchen. 'I've got it, I've got it.'

'Got what, my dear?' she responded, looking up from the washing-up bowl. 'Juliet's surname – it's Mentreath,' blurted out Robert.

'Mentreath? I've known the Mentreaths for years, and you often went to see them when you were younger,' said Hilda.

'They have a daughter called Anne, but I don't recollect a Juliet.' Then it hit her – first names were mainly used by folk around these parts, so they rarely used their other given names, but she recollected Juliet as one of the other given names at Anne's christening. 'That's it,' she said to Robert (who had no middle name), 'Anne Mentreath is Juliet! For some particular faddish reason or other, she is obviously using Juliet now.'

Robert was overjoyed. 'Wonderful,' he exclaimed, 'I'll be able to go and see her now!'

'I tell you what I will do, Robert, we'll go and visit them at Tall Chimneys Farm later this week. I have not seen Alice and Leon for some time, nor Anne and the boys. I used to meet them regularly at church, but what with the difficulties and the ties of the farming life, they often don't get down there these days.'

'Don't you remember,' she went on, 'I used to take you out to the farm to see them when you were younger, and I have certainly taken you and Anne to the seaside together.'

Robert did recall those visits. They were quite exciting on the farm. He recalled less readily the trips to the seaside with Anne. Was it that girl he sat in the back of the car with, her in a summer dress, white ankle socks and sandals, and he in grey flannel short trousers and plimsolls, excited to go to the seaside, with their knees knocking occasionally as the car went round corners. Was that really Juliet?

'I think we will go Thursday afternoon,' said his aunt, interrupting his thoughts.

'They are bound to be in, they rarely stray away from the farmhouse this time of the year. It's not too far into the moor, but difficult to find without a car, and you wouldn't get there easily otherwise,' insisted Hilda.

'That's wonderful, thanks, Aunt,' said Robert, although he would have preferred to have called on his own. But on this first occasion, it would probably be expedient and practical to call for the first time with his aunt.

'Well, that's settled then,' said Hilda, 'go and relax again and I will start preparing for lunch.'

Robert went back to the lounge ecstatic but nervous. Butterflies were in his stomach already. How would Juliet receive him after the debacle of their parting? Would she want to see him again?

Ah well, thought Robert, I've got a couple of days to roam around Bodmin and renew acquaintances before the big day, so I might as well settle down and enjoy myself for the moment.

He leaned back into the comfy armchair, lit another Players, drew heavily, exhaled deeply into the room and relaxed, a contented man.

Chapter Three

Robert awoke abruptly. The discovery from the previous day hit him immediately. Juliet! I will see her in two days' time, on Thursday! He lay back content, musing over all the possibilities that their meeting might bring.

A knock came at the door. 'Come in,' he shouted. His aunt limped in with the rattling tea tray. 'Oh Aunt, you shouldn't, you should not walk up all those stairs bringing tea to me again!'

'Nonsense,' she said, you're on your holidays now after all that work at college, and besides, the exercise keeps me fit.' She didn't add that she liked to do for people, particularly family, and that she was determined to do it anyway!

'Thanks, Aunt,' said Robert.

'Well my dear, what do you intend to do today?'

'I think I'll wander downtown and have a look around the old place to renew my acquaintance with it, and I might try to call in on some of the neighbours and friends if I've got time today – or I will call on them tomorrow.'

'That sounds good my dear, but don't tire yourself out all at once. They know you're down and will expect you to call only when you can.'

'Alright Aunt, I will certainly call on them in due course. I won't rush it though.'

'Well my dear, when you've had your tea come on down for breakfast; Auntie will have a good meal waiting for you.'

Gulp, thought Robert, I'm beginning to eat large breakfasts now – I do hope that I'll be able to walk it off before the obligatory heavy lunch!

She turned on her heel and limped to the door. 'When you are ready,' she said, and closed the door.

Heavens, thought Robert, she's a fine old person. Hilda meant 'battle maid' – a most appropriate name for her!

Robert turned on to his elbow and attended to the early

morning tea in bed ritual. He snapped the Rich Teas, crunched them and washed them down with the brown liquid. He replaced the cup in the saucer with a satisfying porcelain click, twirled the beads on the fascinating tray and swung himself out of bed. Must get ready for the day, he mused. Things to do, people to visit.

He staggered to the bathroom. He thought about his deceased uncle when he observed the razor strop, then he shaved, washed (thank goodness that the geyser was working), returned to his room and dressed.

Robert bounced buoyantly down the stairs, full of nervous expectation as to what the day would bring – and of course with the sustaining anticipation of Thursday, the meeting with Juliet!

Hilda was in full flood, orchestrating the huge breakfast, conducting over the smoking pan.

'We're early today Robert, Miss Mudge has not gone up yet.'

At that moment, a large lorry thundered down Castle Hill just past the kitchen window. 'My,' said Hilda, 'there goes another one, that bypass is a long time coming. We'll be shaken to our foundations before they get on with it.'

'I know,' said Robert, 'lorries of that size should never be allowed through the narrow streets of such a small town.'

'You should see down at the bottom of the hill here, where the lorries turn past St Petroc's. They almost hit the curate's house, they're so close to it. Something must be done soon before they do!'

'I agree Aunt,' said Robert.

'Ah well, it will happen soon enough. Eat up your breakfast now, my dear, before it gets cold.'

Robert ate his large hogs pudding and the rest of his cooked breakfast slowly and thoughtfully. He pondered on his good fortune in being able to stay here with his aunt in this atmospheric house and historical old town, but more particularly on his forthcoming meeting with Juliet. Meanwhile, Hilda had left the kitchen to attend to a knock at the front door, and her excited conversation filtered back to Robert.

Hilda returned to the kitchen. 'A special delivery for you, Robert, from London, and a note from Aunt Aggie asking you to stay with her for a few days in Porth next week.'

'Oh, that's good, Aunt, I'm looking forward to seeing her and all of them down there again – particularly Simeon and John.'

Simeon and John were his cousins but he looked on them as brothers, having played together extensively as boys and more recently maintaining their adult connections and common interests. Porth is the most beautiful and interesting bay in Cornwall, thought Robert, and I know it so well.

'I'll run you down there next week in the car, my dear,' said Hilda, interrupting his thoughts, 'although you may have to come back on the train. I have not seen Aggie for some time and I look forward to going myself!'

'Excellent, Aunt, thanks.' Robert had finished his breakfast by now and was opening his special delivery letter from London. 'That's good,' he exclaimed, 'a note from Dad with a crisp fiver enclosed!'

'What does your dad have to say? How is he, and how is your dear mother?' said Hilda.

'They are fine,' said Robert, 'they send their love, wish they could be down here with us and hope that I will have a good break.' Robert read the rest of the note to her, relating the events that had happened to his parents over the past few weeks and relaying their love to her.

'That's grand,' said Hilda. 'Well, you'd better be getting along now if you are going to see much of the town. If you see anybody I know, remember me to them and say I will either see them down Fore Street 'fore long or at St Petroc's on Sunday or Conservatives on Monday.'

'Fine, Aunt. Is there anything you want from town?'

'No thank you, my dear, just be getting along now. Oh! Lunch will be ready for one o'clock.'

Robert knew not to be late for lunch and left her already in the process of preparing it.

Before leaving the house Robert popped into the lounge, flopped into an armchair and lit up a Players. They were getting low. I'll go to the tobacconist's to get another packet when I am in town, thought Robert. Nothing worse than running out of cigarettes when all the shops are closed! He walked into the hall, grabbed his light raincoat from the hall stand and skipped down the granite steps into the garden and the sloping path past the yew tree to the gate. It was precipitating slightly as it always seemed to in Cornwall in late summer, and he slipped his raincoat on. He swung the gate back, walked through and let it crash back under the pressure of the very strong return spring. Robert walked down to the bottom of Castle Hill, passing Mrs Sandow's and Mrs Cox's dairy on the way past the curate's house towards the entrance steps to St Petroc's church, which faced the *Cornish Guardian* offices on the edge of Honey Street.

Robert paused at the church steps. Just to the right of the steps, and railed off but with access via an iron gate, gushed the spring of water that flowed out from the churchyard. Often in earlier years he had come here with a pitcher in hand to collect the water that flowed here to be placed on his aunt's table for drinking water. It was clear, fresh and cold, and some would say it had medicinal properties and was most suitable for table water. It was sobering to think that this was water from the self-same spring that the original Celtic saint used water from for baptising when he first settled here, centuries before the current Norman church was built.

Robert went to the spring, now emitting from the granite wall marking the boundary of the churchyard, placed his cupped hands into its flow to gather the cold water, sipped some, and spread the rest over his face. He was instinctively performing a baptismal ritual without realising it! Refreshed, he stepped back and thought, Shall I go into the church or continue on into the town? The church always had a pull on him and he spontaneously leapt up the steps, waving his hands through the air to dry them, walked past St Guron's well (caged in) and along the church path to the main entrance.

Entering the church, he was immediately enveloped in its peaceful atmosphere, away from the busyness of the main road just outside. He was always impressed by the 'retired' military flags of the local regiment, the Duke of Cornwall's Light Infantry, deposited there for safekeeping. The worn and threadbare banners hung from their ceiling positions still and silent, hiding their military glories from the casual passer-by. The ancient carved Norman baptismal font stood sentinel at the back of the church, attesting to the numerous Christian baptisms administered there long after the baptisms in the churchyard spring had ceased. The twelfth-century ivory reliquary casket, once containing the relics of St Petroc, at the window alcove in the right-hand aisle was an object of great fascination to him.

Robert moved to the sanctuary area and to the Bible placed on the lectern, open to display the Gospel reading for the day. He read, 'Seek ye first the Kingdom of God and all these things shall be added unto you.' Where exactly is God's Kingdom? thought Robert. He walked out of the main door and circumvented the building to the rear of the church and to the little ruined chapel at the back. This chapel was part of the original church of the monastic foundation that Bodmin (abode of monks) was formed from. This post-Reformation ruin remained and to Robert was a source of mystical inspiration. Not well known to many, it was a quiet spot and an ideal place for peaceful contemplation and meditation. But time had not been kind to it. It was bereft of a roof and its arched windows had long lost their stained glass. It had the remains of an altar stone, and Robert could imagine old church celebrations and rituals being enacted here, although he was not particularly certain as to their exact purpose.

Refreshed, he left the chapel, walked back around the main church building to the steps by the spring, rapidly skipped down them and crossed the road towards Honey Street. As he crossed, he noticed a stationary AA motorcycle combination in the parking area outside the fishing tackle shop towards which he was heading. The AA patrolman was leaning nonchalantly against the combination, smoking a cigarette. His gauntlet gloves, helmet and goggles were resting on the seat of the motorcycle as he puffed away at his cigarette. Robert observed him more closely, from his steel-studded boots, calf-hugging black leather gaiters to his khaki brown serge uniform. It must be awfully hot wearing all that, thought Robert, particularly in summer, although he realised on a motorbike you were very exposed and a wind resistant material was vital.

As he approached, something very familiar about the patrolman became apparent. Goodness, thought Robert, it's Mr Burton – I have not seen him for years. He had stayed with Robert's aunt years ago when she was first widowed, and out of necessity at the time had rented rooms for income before his late uncle's affairs had been settled. His uncle's estate took a long time to organise, as being an auctioneer, he dabbled in many other activities connected to local estates, and it took a long time to track down all his additional monetary sources!

'Hello, Mr Burton, do you remember me?' Robert said as he approached him.

The patrolman looked up, quizzically scrutinized Robert's face and said, 'Well, can't say I do.'

'You stayed at my aunt's, Mrs Yudy's, a few years ago when you first came to Cornwall – I was a lot younger then. I'm Robert, by the way.'

'Well that was some time ago,' replied Mr Burton. 'I do remember a young Robert there, he was quite an adventurous lad. How is Mrs Yudy? I have not seen her for a few years, and you are certainly grown-up now.'

'She is fine, and still living at 7 Castle Hill.'

'One day I ought to call in on her, but these days my patrol activities don't often bring me into Bodmin town.'

Their conversation flowed for a while, Mr Burton recollecting how lucky he was, post-war and discharged from the army, to get an AA patrolman's job, and Robert saying how fascinated he was when riding in the aunt's car and watching the approach of an AA motorcycle combination. You would wait for the snappy open-handed salute proffered by the patrolman, but only if your car was sporting the AA badge.

'Well, I must be getting on,' said Mr Burton, crushing his cigarette butt beneath the heel of a mighty studded boot. He put on his helmet, fixed the goggles on the helmet brim and pulled on his gauntlets. Then he mounted the BSA motorcycle, gave a smart salute to Robert, kick-started the machine, revved his engine, gave Robert a great grin, saying 'duty calls,' and pulled away in a cloud of smoke. Robert raised his hand in acknowledgement and watched him cruise down Priory Road towards Launceston, Liskeard and Plymouth.

It was good to have seen him, thought Robert. Interesting character – wonder if I will see him again? He turned his attention to the window of the fishing tackle shop. These places always fascinated him, with their copious quantities of rods, lines, hooks, flies, floats and tackle to suit every form of fishing in the area. Robert's aunt had taught him to fish, particularly for the local river and stream brown trout. She used brandling worms and not fly, and brought in many a catch. The licensing situation was benevolent in the area, needing only a river-board area licence and perhaps the farmer's permission to cross his land to the river.

Robert entered the shop and browsed around. There were some magnificent split cane rods there and some excellent free-running centre pin reels for fly-fishing, an activity that one day Robert thought he might take up. Meanwhile, he would stick to the more mundane, but just as effective, methods he was brought up with.

'Can I help you, sir?' came the Cornish burr of the shopkeeper.

'Thank you,' said Robert 'but I'm just browsing. Although I may try and get a bit of fishing in down at Respryn during my stay here if I have time.'

'You'll need a river-board licence for that, you know, sir,' came the firm reply.

'How much are they now?' said Robert.

'Five pounds for the season or ten shillings for a fortnight,' replied the man.

That's not too bad for a fortnight, thought Robert. 'How is the fishing down there at the moment?'

'Very good,' was the reply. 'The water is high due to the recent rain and some good catches are reported, up to three and a half pounds.'

'That *is* good,' said Robert, 'for that particular stretch. Light tackle with ones that size and they will give you a run for your money.'

''Ess, they certainly will and they be such good eating after-wards,' chuckled the man. 'Nothing like 'em!'

'Well, thanks,' said Robert. 'I'll call again when I can be certain of going and I will buy some tackle. Cheerio then.'

'Bye bye then,' said the man, 'I hope you can return. Enjoy your stay otherwise.'

Robert walked out of the shop. The door rattled shut behind him and he set off up Honey Street. He glanced at his watch. Eleven o'clock already. My, time has flown, and I have hardly started, thought Robert, being very conscious of the 1 p.m. lunch deadline. He proceeded to the top end of Honey Street, crossed over the road and passed the fish and chip shop. Excellent fish and chips from there, particularly after coming out from the cinema at night. On this side of Honey Street he came to the grocery store. He knew that his aunt shopped here for all her groceries, and decided to go to see Jack Bray the grocer, and wondered whether or not he would recognise him. Jack Bray was a long-standing friend, known to his mother as well as his aunt, although where the relationship originated from, he barely knew, only that he was regarded with great affection.

Robert entered the store and the shop bell rang. A couple of ladies, clutching shopping bags, were conversing with the grocer, who looked up as the bell went. 'Morning sir, what can I do for you?'

The ladies moved away slightly from the counter to allow Robert to approach, but they did not depart from the shop. He knew that they were taking him in. If you were new in town you were noticed! 'Hello Jack, do you remember me I'm Hilda Yudy's nephew, Robert.'

'My, boy, is it you? How you've grown,' said Jack. The ladies perked up interest and stayed to overhear the conversation.

Robert glanced around the store and looked at the shelves laden with all kinds of produce: sugar, tea, bread, cheese under a glass cover, and particularly the bacon and ham slicer on the marble counter.

The bacon slicer had always fascinated Robert. He used to marvel at the thinness of the slices coming off when he was a boy and then Jack would say, 'Here boy, try a bit of this ham – it's good for you.'

'Yes Jack, I'm back again, staying with Aunt for a couple of weeks. It's nice to be here again.'

'Lovely to see you again boy. How is your mother Winnie?'

Robert suspected that in the past, Jack had had a soft spot for his mother when they were young, but she had been whisked away to London by his father and that was that! Jack had never married. Robert recounted all the events of recent years and the current family situation. Jack listened attentively and the ladies marvelled that Robert was Mrs Yudy's nephew and what an ''andsom' young man he was. Jack remembered when Robert used to play in Hilda's garden; walking past to and fro between the store and home he would often stop and talk to Robert.

After a pleasant chat, Robert said that he must be moving on. 'Lovely to see you again boy, call in again when you can.'

The ladies said, 'Hope to see you again,' and Robert walked out of the store, the doorbell clanging behind him.

He turned left and proceeded up to Fore Street past the town clock set in its granite tower. It chimed eleven thirty just as he passed. Time is moving on, thought Robert, clutching for a cigarette. He paused and lit it, noticing the bijou cinema on the right. He had spent quite a few Saturday evenings there in the past, sitting in the only main row, smoking copiously and watching the black and white films on the square silver screen. The local boys and girls used to cuddle up in the back rows or where they could. Happy days, thought Robert, if somewhat solitary for him. A bag of chips well laced with salt and vinegar on the way back to his aunt's had put a good seal on many a cinema evening in the past!

He continued higher up into Fore Street past Tolworth's the tailors, where all a gentleman's clothing and accoutrements could be purchased, and on to find the tobacconist's.

There it was, further up on the left-hand side. He went through the door, the bell jangled and the full tobacconist's array was before him. The pipes in racks, the stacked cigarette packets of every popular brand and some obscure, the bowls of pipe tobacco, ready mixed and pre-packeted, buy and rub your own or have a mix made up for you. Robert had tried a pipe occasionally and St Bruno or Three Nuns was his favourite. The bead curtain from the back entrance rustled and parted, and the proprietor entered.

'Good morning sir, and what can I do for you?'

'I would like a packet of twenty Players medium please.'

'Yes sir.' The packet of Players was proffered over the counter and the proprietor said, 'two shillings and sixpence please, sir.'

Robert searched in his trouser pocket, pulled out a handful of coins and selected a florin, a three penny bit and three pennies and handed them to the man.

'Thank you sir exactly! Would sir like anything else?'

'Not at the moment, thank you. Good morning,' and Robert left the shop. He crossed over Fore Street and continued his walk on to the top end of the town.

Soon he came to the shop in town that had the most enduring memories for him. It was Bricknell's, the toyshop! Every holiday he had spent at his aunt's in the past he had been provided with pocket money. Furnished by his father and his uncle, it allowed him financial scope to purchase a holiday toy, and Bricknell's was the only destination in town in which to find such things. As a lad, his favourite purchase was that of a new cowboy gun. Heavens knows what happened to the previous year's purchases – he could only surmise that they had become mislaid or broken and were consigned to the dustbin! Often such purchases were exotic (to him) in that the cowboy revolvers were increasingly authentic and well produced, imitating the actual revolvers seen in the films. The best one, one year, had a dual barrel with a revolving chamber which dummy bullets could be inserted into and removed from, as well as the traditional rolled cap firing mechanism. Robert had had tremendous fun with it, charging round his aunt's house, banging off reels of caps at imaginary foes – much to the consternation of his uncle, who even then was ailing, and Robert did not understand his desire for peace and quiet!

Robert hesitated in front of the shop. He glimpsed in the shop windows at the toys and books on display and beyond, to the long illuminated interior. Nothing much seemed to have changed; it still held the promise of exciting purchases, even an interesting paperback read. However, he thought, on another occasion, when I have more time. He glanced at his watch – ten to twelve already. He determined to push on. He entered Bore Street, walked up past the Walker VC estate from where he could just observe the towers of the old jail, and continued to the roundabout between Westheath Avenue and Dunmere Road. This was the limit of his morning's walk. To continue further on was to go further west into Cornwall and to the right led along the Camel River to Wadebridge.

St Lawrence's hospital, colloquially known as the Asylum, lay to the right and served the whole of Cornwall, and directly ahead was the Catholic church. No time to visit now, but its abbey style had always attracted him to call in and explore its hidden interior or at least to explore what was actually different within a Catholic church!

Pushed for time now, Robert turned on his heel and headed back into town. He retraced his steps through Bore Street onto Fore Street and diverted past the town hall towards Priory Park. I've just got time to do a whirl of the priory grounds before going back to my aunt's, he thought. He entered the grounds past the duck pond that probably had been the monastic fish pond, past two ruined monks' cells that were still standing after all the centuries that had passed, and that brought him back to St Petroc's. He crossed the road, entered the church grounds via the rear gate, skirted the main church and retraced his steps to the main entrance stairs and to the spring. I wonder how many gallons of water have poured through there since my circuit of the town? he thought. If I knew the rate of flow and the diameter of the orifice, I'm sure I could do the calculation, he mused. He arrested the thought immediately. No 'shop' whilst on holiday was his self-imposed rule!

He glanced at his watch. It was twelve thirty. I've got a bit of time before I need to be back, he thought, I don't want to arrive too early. I'll look in on Mrs Cox briefly before going back. By now, the sun had come out and it was getting warm. Robert removed his raincoat and folded it over his arm. He crossed the road at the bottom of Castle Hill and entered Cox's Dairy through its open door. He walked over the flagstoned floor and the dairy smell was all-pervading. Mrs Cox was busy, with her back to the counter, filling containers of all shapes and sizes with clotted cream. She seemed oblivious to the fact that anyone had entered and it wasn't until Robert coughed in the dairy's cool atmosphere that she turned to him. 'Good morning m'dear, what can I do for 'ee?'

'Hello Mrs Cox, I'm Robert, staying with Mrs Yudy on Castle Hill. I just popped in to say hello to you while I'm down.'

'Robert, my, you have grown, my dear, lovely to see you again. How be you getting on then?'

Robert gave her chapter and verse as to what he had been doing and she responded about life down at the dairy, saying that business was 'adequate my dear, adequate'.

'Your auntie still pops in here for her cream and Bobby still delivers her milk. Mind you, she has to be careful getting down here on wet days, with her leg and all that.'

Bobby Cox was her son who had Downs Syndrome. He was the ideal person to help with the local milk delivery.

'How is Bobby?' said Robert.

'Oh, he is about as fine as he can be, but a bit mazed sometimes when he gets confused. I'm getting older and I've really no one to take it all on after me. Bobby can't, but there we are my dear; all good things come to an end sooner or later, don't they!'

Robert mumbled some sympathetic words and then said, 'I will have to go now, Aunt has lunch for me at one o'clock and it's nearly that now and I must not be late.'

'Your auntie will feed you up well my dear, she makes a proper job of cooking, a real proper job.'

'Bye now Mrs Cox, I hope to see you again, and to see Bobby around sometime.'

Robert crossed the road, went up Castle Hill and reached his aunt's gate. The church clock started chiming one o'clock as he sprinted up the path past the yew tree over the granite steps and into the hall via the open front door.

'Is that you my dear? Come into the kitchen, lunch is ready,' called out Hilda.

The lunch was enormous, a beef stew with vegetables followed by apple pie with clotted cream. Robert felt bloated with food and it was about all he could do to stagger to the lounge and collapse into an armchair, having been ordered by Hilda to do so. 'No, no, I'll clear up,' she said, 'you go and have a read of the newspaper and see what the world is doing. I'll join you for a chat in the lounge later.'

They chatted that afternoon about what Robert had done and

whom he had seen, and Hilda came in with various aspects and tales of family history and what the neighbours had been doing lately. The afternoon wore on, and Robert felt too tired for any more visits today. The afternoon sped by rapidly under these conditions and amazingly it was time for tea in no time at all! Robert insisted, 'Just a cup of tea please, Aunt,' but was persuaded to eat Cornish splits with strawberry jam and cream, followed by saffron cake. They sat chatting in the lounge until the church curfew bell tolled at 8 p.m. and the town was silent. Robert would have liked to have gone out for a walk to ease off all the food he had eaten, but there was really nowhere to go in the town at night, so he stayed put, smoking and conversing with his aunt until it was time for bed.

Chapter Four

Robert awoke and slowly came to his senses as he opened his eyes and adjusted to the early morning gloom of the room. What day is it today? he thought, awareness of where he was slowly catching up with him. Ah, it's Wednesday, another day to get through prior to tomorrow's meeting with Juliet. The thoughts of that meeting filtered through his brain and its anticipation was already giving him butterflies in his stomach. I do hope that I won't get too nervy on the day, he mused, and make a tongue-tied fool of myself. He comforted himself with the thought that Juliet had a warm sympathetic nature and that he was sure that any faux pas he might make would be absorbed by her kindly nature and overlooked. Well, I must not dwell on the possibilities too long, he thought as experience had taught him that practice often was very different to theoretical speculation as to how things might be! He drifted back into a very relaxed sleep.

Dong, dong, dong... The church bell striking the hour of eight o'clock woke him abruptly. He lay there listening to the tolling. Its deep, resonant booming always filled him with awe and a sense of his own frailty against such a mighty summons. He had always liked the sound of church bells tolling or in peals. They were so unique, epitomising a thorough Englishness, as though calling the nation to be one under St George's banner. He thought of that wonderful film, *For Whom the Bell Tolls,* which he had seen in London, with the riveting performances of Gary Cooper and Ingrid Bergman, how impressive it was... His thought pattern was interrupted by a knocking at the door. It was his aunt again with the tea. There was no stopping Hilda with the early morning tea delivery!

Robert went down fairly rapidly for breakfast. He was not so tired in the mornings by now, as the rest and relaxation were doing him good, particularly his reasonably early night yesterday.

The giant breakfast was placed before him and he began to

tuck in. He was getting used to them by now and was thinking that one day he would miss them. Cornish relatives always had a habit of feeding you up well, considering it most important for one's health! He remembered seeing an old postcard displaying Cornish fare on a table that literally groaned with food, from pasties and potato pie through to saffron and yeast cake. This was no exaggeration, as his aunt's table often reflected this. It was pretty heavy stuff! They weren't over-indulgent, but an independent, generous people used to working a hard land, translating their labour into that most important thing: produce!

Hilda broke into his thoughts. 'When you were out yesterday, I did call in on Mrs Sandow and the Bunts briefly, to remind them that you were staying down here and that you might call in on them today.'

'Yes that's all right, Aunt, I look forward to seeing them again,' said Robert.

'You'd better be calling on them after lunch,' insisted Hilda. 'They're a bit particular about visiting times, being of the old school. I'm going downtown this morning to do a bit of shopping, and so we'll have a cold lunch today.'

'Would you like me to go to town to get anything for you this morning?' asked Robert.

'No, no,' said Hilda, 'I have to go; some groceries to buy and some bills to pay.' Robert knew that she would also be having a good old chinwag with her friends and acquaintances, and would not miss an opportunity to go, particularly while she was still so active. 'You rest up my dear, have a look through Auntie's books and have a good read – I know that you are partial to one.'

The front doorbell jangled. Good, the bell pull still operated then, thought Robert since he had repaired the wire linkage on a previous stay.

'Get that will you, my dear, while I clear up the breakfast things, thank 'ee.'

Robert left the kitchen, walked along the hall and opened the front door. A small man looked up at him from the bottom of the doorstep. He was wearing a brown trilby and his grey flannel trousers were tucked into his socks that emerged from his ankle-tied hobnailed boots. His shirt was white with blue stripes, open-necked and collarless. His midriff was encased in a waistcoat, from the right-hand pocket of which emerged the fob of a watch, and he was wearing a pinstriped jacket, quite worn and shiny in places.

'Morning,' he said, 'for Mrs Yudy,' and proffered a wicker basket laden with garden produce. They were magnificent vegetables, long runner beans, carrots, potatoes and some curly cabbage.

Robert took the handle of the basket and said, 'Thank you. Who shall I say called?'

'Lobb,' he said, 'Silus Lobb.' Recognition dawned across Robert's face. 'Oh, I know, Mr Lobb from down near the old jail, I remember visiting you when I was younger. I'm Robert and I'm staying with Aunt Hilda for two or three weeks.'

'Pleased to see you again boy, enjoying your stay I hope? Tell your aunt that I'll be getting on with tidying up her garden shortly.'

That's it, thought Robert, he is a great gardener and that produce is from his own garden. He recollected seeing the garden in the past and even as a young boy, generally uninterested in such things, he was really impressed by the magnificent growth of Mr Lobb's vegetable plot. In fact, it took up almost the whole garden, with little room for anything else. So he is now doing some gardening for Aunt, Robert thought. She does need some help to keep it tidy. He was sure Mr Lobb enjoyed the work and undoubtedly earned a few bob in the process!

Mr Lobb said 'I'm just off to town to get some baccy for m'pipe and I'll be back shortly for the gardening. Can't work properly without a pipe. Cheerio for now.' He turned and walked slowly down the garden path with his undulating gait. It's incredible how he keeps going, thought Robert, at his age too.

Robert returned to the kitchen. Hilda had just finished the washing-up in the white enamelled bowl on the table and was just squeezing out the dishcloth to dry. She walked over to replace the packet of soap flakes in the cupboard next to the sink. 'Who was it, my dear?' she said. She turned and saw the basket of vegetables held in Robert's hand. 'Glory be,' she exclaimed, 'thank the Lord for small mercies! Was it Mr Lobb then?' she said, recognising the basket. 'I must make him and Mrs Lobb a pasty each for next time I see 'em. Silas is so kind.'

'It was Mr Lobb all right, Aunt,' said Robert. 'He will start the gardening soon but he had to go to town for some tobacco.'

Hilda chuckled. ''Ess, that's Silas all right, can't do too much without a pipe in his mouth all day!'

'Well, go off then, my dear, and sit yourself down,' she said, taking the vegetable basket from him. 'I'll just pop these into the pantry and get myself ready for going to town. I'll probably be passing Silas coming back from town, if I don't get a move on.'

Outside the kitchen door and across the hall was the sunken pantry to the right of the steps leading to the cellar. The pantry was large, flagstoned and cool. It contained all sorts of pots and pans and produce, like cheese, milk and bread and ham, and was used even to hang the odd pheasant or two in when Hilda became the recipient of the catch from a local shoot. She placed the vegetables into the vegetable rack and went upstairs to change for her trip to town.

Robert walked through to the lounge, chose his favourite armchair by the fireplace and collapsed into it. He pulled out a cigarette from the packet he had left on the coffee table from last night and struck the red-topped match on the serrated edge of the silver matchbox holder. Robert lit the cigarette and inhaled deeply, and discarded the spent matchstick into the grate.

Robert thought that things were not going too badly really – just today to get through, and then he would see Juliet tomorrow. He was already thinking of a follow-up strategy to meet her another time. But where? Perhaps a tea room or a pub. Transport would pose a problem, or in fact, the lack of it would! How could he pick her up from the farm for a subsequent meeting without transport? He knew that buses would be almost impossible and he could not keep prevailing on his aunt for lifts, no matter how willing she would be. One needed a bit of privacy with a girl anyhow. Well, for the moment I will put it out of my mind, he thought. We still have Thursday to get through yet!

Robert puffed away on his cigarette and looked thoughtfully out of the window across the garden towards the church tower. What should he do before lunch and the afternoon visits? He stubbed out the cigarette, rose to his feet and walked across the hallway to the dining room. Since his arrival he had not been in the dining room. Aunt did not eat in there unless the occasion was deemed to be formal, with a number of visiting guests. Farming friends would certainly merit a formal dinner, as would the vicar and his wife and the curate. The Websters, a country gentry family from Bradley Manner, Newton Abbot with which the family had ties, would particularly merit the most formal of occasions. They did not visit that often due to the distances involved, but the mutual regard between the families was still very strong, with Hilda being the main letter writer and preserver of the link. Robert remembered their visits from the past and how he had to mind very much his Ps and Qs in their presence. There was no question that this was expected of him. His grandmother had been the ladies' maid and minor governess to Misses Isabel and Elise, neither of whom had married, and when Robert met them, they seemed rather eccentric and tweedy. Captain Webster RN, their brother was a man's man with a reasonably distinguished war career, and Aunt Hilda held him in high esteem. He did talk rather eccentrically though, and reminded Robert of a raconteur from the 'Brains Trust'. Robert supposed that the captain's upbringing and schooling had created this particular persona for him, and he was captive to it. Their fortunes had changed post-war somewhat with their investments on the decline. However, they still tried to live 'according to their station'. They were very charming people.

Robert entered the dining room. It was very Victorian. Directly across in the left-hand corner of the room was a large bureau full of old, interesting books. Immediately to the left was a large sideboard with its built-in wine cooler cabinets. The decanters for holding sherry and wine were sitting on the silver tray on top of the sideboard. Mounted on the wall above was that interesting black and white print, 'The Rent Day', depicting tenants lining up at a landlord's table to pay their rent, with some characters ravenously eating chops in the general melee of the scene. Directly ahead was an open fireplace with a black marble surround. Georgian candlesticks were on the mantelpiece either side of the Victorian bracket clock, along with brass plates and ornaments of eastern origin. Covering the open grate was a vertically angled Indian brass table-top, conveniently substituting for a fire screen. Everything was polished and the overall effect was very attractive.

To the immediate right of the open door was a magnificent American desk. With its massive doors swung open and the desktop down, rows and rows of small drawers and cubby holes were on display, holding many an interesting item, from Victorian postcards to Georgian coins. His uncle had used the desk for filing his business papers and for writing at. Robert had always explored this desk for interesting artefacts and his aunt often allowed him to keep the occasional item when he visited.

Filling the centre of the room was the massive Victorian table and chairs at which the 'formal' dinners were conducted. The chairs were rather a penance to sit at, with unyielding straight backs and cushions stuffed with horsehair that proved uncomfortable to sit on when the stiff bristles punctured through the covering fabric to penetrate the clothing of your rear end!

Robert walked over to the large bureau and surveyed the book spines through the glass panels of the doors. The books he knew were all still there. Over the years, on previous visits, he had spent a long time going through as many of them as he could. What else would a studious lad do, with a fair amount of time to kill, in a quiet town such as Bodmin? His gaze swept over the book spines. Fairly early editions of *The Complete Angler* by Isaac Walton and *The Pilgrims Progress* by John Bunyan. A Victorian medical dictionary with bizarre illustrations, an early edition of Mrs Beeton's cookery book, *Cornish Saints and Sinners*, *West Country Journeys*, *The Mighty Atom* by Marie Corelli and *Droll Stories* by Balzac. These were just a few of them and many of the others were about hunting, shooting and fishing pursuits in Scotland, the West Country and elsewhere. Robert, as mentioned, had avidly read most of them and skipped through many of the others. When he was younger, he had regretted reading Balzac's *Droll Stories*, as some of the tales were quite disturbing, and on going to bed he had feared switching off the light and trying to go to sleep. Even the medical dictionary had disturbed him with its description of particular complaints and one particular illustration of a young baby born covered in hair! Now as an adult, such things were not so disturbing, but still very interesting.

Robert took *The Complete Angler* off the shelf and returned to the lounge. He settled into the armchair, lit a cigarette and opened the book. It was a fascinating insight into the gentlemanly angling pursuits of Isaac Walton, with all the descriptions of the tackle and the methods used. Particularly interesting was the hospitality shown in the countryside in Walton's day to travelling gentlemen who pursued such pursuits and the agreeable conversations with similar-minded fellows.

Robert had been through the book many times before and he was just renewing his acquaintance with it, and so was skipping through fairly rapidly. The church clock struck eleven o'clock. Robert looked up and could just make out the clock face in the lounge, but not the hands. Eleven, he mused, Aunt probably won't be back from town until about twelve.

He grew tired of reading and put the book down. These days he could not read for quite such long periods as he used to. Perhaps it was all that studying he did at college. It has probably killed off my desire to follow a book for such a long time, he thought. He crushed out his cigarette in the ashtray and looked out of the window into the garden. The sun had come out and it was a glorious day. Hopefully it should hold for the visit to Juliet tomorrow. Mr Lobb had returned from town and Robert could see him pottering about the garden, gathering dead sticks from plants and stacking them in a small wheelbarrow.

I know what I will do, he thought, I'll have a mooch around the cellar and see if it still looks the same.

He got up, went through the lounge doorway, turned left into the hall and along to the cellar door under the stairs.

He pulled back the cellar door, switched on the light and made his way down the narrow, winding stone stairs, holding on to the wooden rail. The cellar smell hit him – a dankness combined with aged, still air. The cellar floor was flagstoned and in the far right-hand corner was an old copper boiler for clothes and household linen, long since fallen into disuse. Further to the right in an alcove was the coal hole and chute down which the coal would be poured from the street outside into the coal bunker situated at the bottom of the chute.

He moved across to the cellar windows facing out towards the front of the house. The view was partially obscured due to the dirt and grime of ages, and one's eyes were level with the surface of the front garden. It was quite amusing – he could see the boots and legs of Mr Lobb up to knee level, walking around the garden as though disembodied. Up on the wall between the windows was a wooden board, to which was fixed the remains of springs of old bronze bells for calling up the servants. Did servants really have to live and work in these cellar conditions of yesteryear? he thought. It must have been pretty hard in those days, he mused. Who would really want to sleep in this damp cellar? Perhaps they were just day servants – a visiting cook maybe, and a household maid perhaps.

Robert remembered the cellar well; he had often played down here with his cowboy cap guns and had even tried his first pipe down here without his parents and aunt knowing. How they did not pick up the smell of the tobacco smoke, he did not know!

He turned to walk out of the cellar, noticing the main ceiling beam supports for the house still with hooks on, which his aunt and uncle had stored their fishing rods and hung the old fishing catgut up to dry out, having washed them in fresh water to clear the salt from the line after sea fishing. If not washed, the old gut line would go brittle and easily snap in use the next time.

Robert left the cellar, re-entered the hall and went to the front door and opened it. The sun streamed in, lighting up the hall and throwing up the colours of the hunting prints to much richer depths.

'Hello Mr Lobb, get your tobacco all right?'

''Ess thank'ee boy, and it's smoking well,' he said clenching his pipe between his teeth. 'Saw Mrs Yudy downtown – she'll be back 'fore too long.'

Mr Lobb turned to his tasks and Robert sat down on the steps and basked in the sun. He was fascinated by the glinting of the mica in the granite rocks surrounding the garden borders as they were illuminated by the sun, and went into a semi-comatose state of peaceful recollection, seemingly without a care in the world. He had sat here on many a previous occasion and delighted in the peacefulness of it all. He decided against another cigarette just yet.

The bang of the front gate penetrated his contemplative state and he opened his eyes to see his aunt limping up the garden path carrying her shopping bag. 'I see that you've been making good progress, Silas,' she said to Mr Lobb. 'It's looking a lot better. How have you been getting on, Robert?'

'Fine, Aunt, had a good read.'

'I'm glad you find those books so interesting my dear, Uncle Percy was a great reader like you.' Robert jumped up and took the shopping bag from her and followed her into the kitchen. 'Well, I will prepare a bit of lunch for us in a minute or two.'

'Would you like a cup of tea before you start, Aunt?'

'That would be very nice, thank you.' Robert made a pot for two and Hilda said, 'Ask Mr Lobb if he would like one too'.

Robert returned from asking Mr Lobb and gave Hilda his answer. 'He said no thanks as he is reserving that space for something special a little later on.'

Hilda chuckled. 'I know what he's reserving that for. He'll be down the Hole in the Wall later, drinking beer with the old boys in the corner of the bar!'

They finished their tea and Hilda started making preparations for lunch. Robert went upstairs to his room for a freshen-up. Hilda called upstairs, 'Come down when you're ready my dear, lunch is ready.'

The lunch was a light one today. Excellent local cured ham carved into enormous slices, served with boiled potatoes, beetroot and tomato chutney, and baked bread rolls with rich yellow butter, both local. The pudding was cold fruit, apple and locally picked blackberries mixed topped with enormous helpings of clotted cream. There was even a Cornish split to follow!

'That was excellent, Aunt thank you,' said Robert. 'I'm quite full now and can't manage any more!' The lunchtime conversation had been rambling over many topics and on whom Hilda had seen in town and what they had been getting up to lately.

'Well, I'll clear up now,' said Hilda, 'and you'll be popping out to see the neighbours this afternoon.'

'Yes,' said Robert. 'I'll just rest a bit to let the lunch go down and then I'll be going across.'

'All right my dear.'

Robert went to the lounge, collapsed into the chair and nodded off for a bit.

Dong, dong! Robert awoke with a start. Heavens, he thought, is it two o'clock already? I'd better go and visit before it gets too late!

Robert walked hurriedly out of the house. I'll call in on Mrs Sandow first, he thought. She lived across the road from Aunt Hilda and her spinster daughter, Miss Sandow, lived with her. Mrs Sandow had been married to a wine merchant and was widowed, and now lived quietly at home with her daughter.

Robert rang the doorbell and waited – it seemed for an eternity. After the noise of sliding bolts and rattling chains, the door finally opened, displaying Mrs Sandow in a long black dress with white lace cuffs and a rather heavy diamond pendant at her neck. Her cheeks were very rouged in contrast to her white curled hair.

'It's Robert is it, Mrs Yudy's nephew? Do come in, I've been expecting you.'

She conducted him to the dark, Victorian parlour, emitting the quality of being 'well to do' although a little tarnished by the number of elapsed years.

'Its nice to see you again Mrs Sandow, I have not seen you for some time.'

'I understand, Robert, that you have just finished at university and are expecting an honours degree; that is very good.'

'Yes I am,' replied Robert, 'although it was a lot of hard work getting through the course.'

'I'm sure that will get you into a fine job in no time at all,' she said.

'I hope so,' said Robert, eager to change the subject. 'How is Skip, by the way?'

'Poor old Skip, I had to have him put down. He was getting very old and his bowels were failing.'

'I'm sorry to hear that,' said Robert. He remembered Skip, a funny little dog that he used to walk for her around Priory Park. It was of the schipperke breed that apparently originated from Belgium in the 1600s and was bred as a barge-watching ratter, the breed name meaning 'little captain' in English. It was largely disregarded by the English aristocracy as a non-sporting dog and

Robert often wondered how she came to find such a dog. He used to be quite embarrassed taking it around Priory Park, as the local ruffian kids would make disparaging remarks about it and refer to it as a cat or a rat on a lead!

'Would you like a glass of something, Robert?'

'Well, thank you, I would,' Robert answered, knowing that it was rude to refuse.' He knew what was coming – he had been through this ritual many times before when visiting with his mother, although then he was offered only orange squash!

She reached to the chair-side cabinet and reached out two cut glass goblets and a decanter of the reddest-looking wine you could imagine. She poured out generous quantities in the two goblets and offered one to him, and he took it and began to sip. 'Thank you, very nice,' he said, belying the fact it was a little insipid. It was a family joke that she proffered VP wine, a very basic English wine, known jokingly as Very Poor from its initials on the bottle. However, the family was never to know officially, as she always offered it decanted! It was rather strange, he thought, as her husband had been a wine merchant and he must have introduced her to better quality wine than this.

The parlour door opened and in walked Miss Sandow, her daughter. She was looking very spinsterish and dowdy, probably now approaching fifty and still a companion to her mother. Mrs Sandow introduced them and Robert stood to shake her hand.

'Have a glass with us, Jane,' said her mother.

'No thank you, mother,' she replied, 'I've just had some tea and besides, as you know, I am not keen on wine anyway,' she said by way of rebuke.

Robert sensed the atmosphere of resentment and found this type of situation incredibly sad. She had probably missed chances of marriage in years gone by and ended up being her mother's companion and helpmate. Her main outlet was playing the church organ out at St Neot's on the moor, a lovely church with magnificent fifteenth-century stained glass windows. It was a mystery how she got out there for Sunday services and for practice, as they had no car!

Robert said some cheery words to her and noticed that she coloured up and made an excuse to return to the kitchen. 'Ah well, Mrs Sandow, thank you for the hospitality. I really must be getting on. It's been interesting talking to you again and I'm sorry about poor old Skip, I used to like taking him out for walks, as you know. Cheerio now.'

'Bye bye,' said Mrs Sandow as she closed the front door and Robert heard the bolts being slid across.

After a short leap across the road Robert entered his aunt's garden and took the path to Mrs Bunt's house, the second in the curved bow of houses next door to Aunt Hilda's. There was no gate and so he walked straight through to the door.

Knock, knock. He banged on the door using the ornate door-knocker. A shuffling was heard the other side of the door before it opened. Mrs Bunt opened the door. She looked every inch the elderly Edwardian lady from her lace cap to her long flowing dress.

'Robert! I've been expecting you,' she said, and bent her head over to receive a kiss.

Robert leaned over to kiss her on the cheek but met her chin lower down and had to contend with bristly whiskers! 'Your auntie has told me so much about you and what you have been doing lately. She is so proud of you,' she said as she led him into the front reception room of the house.

It was comfortably furnished and he sat in an armchair at her direction. She sat on the sofa, leaving plenty of room for the arrival of her sister. Robert noticed the print of the Royal Horse Artillery gun team at the gallop in the First World War was still on the wall facing him, and he remembered that her husband had been a major in that regiment. He had vague memories of being bounced up and down on his knee as a young boy to the song of 'Here Comes the Galloping Major'. The sepia photograph on the table showed him as a younger man in his khaki uniform, very smart, with a shiny Sam Browne across his chest. Mrs Bunt noticed Robert looking at the photograph. 'Yes,' she said wistfully, 'he was a very smart man,' as though reading Robert's thoughts!

'Well, we will have some tea,' she said, as though anticipating the arrival of her sister walking through the door with the rattling tea tray, laden with pot, cups and scones. 'Come and sit next to me Gwen,' she said.

Robert stood up and greeted Gwen, who was almost a replica of her sister, but younger. He found her chin not quite so hairy. She had never married and as was customary in those days, the unmarried female often lived with the married couple – where would she have gone otherwise? They were now elderly companions for one another, but so often the unmarried one played the role of the servant as she had no income of her own.

The tea was good and the scones with strawberry jam and cream were delicious. The conversation struggled on until the exhaustion of all topics and Robert knew when to make his move. The Bunts would have kept him on much longer, relishing his company, but he made his excuses that his aunt was expecting him for tea (how he would eat tea after this he did not know), and managed to extricate himself with honour from the fray. He made his goodbyes and retreated to the door, thanking them very much and saying that he would love to call again.

He walked down the path to his aunt's house and entered via the open front door.

'Is that you, Robert?' called his aunt from the lounge. Robert went in and found Hilda with her reading glasses on, her foot resting on the foot-stool, reading the *Western Morning News*. She took her glasses off, put the newspaper down in her lap, squinted at him and said, 'How did you get on with them, then?'

Robert explained all the proceedings and she listened attentively to all the news, interjecting with the occasional ''ess' and 'that's right my dear,' and she chuckled at some of the described behaviour. 'Well, you know how they are my dear – like a lot of old Dame Trots, don't expect anything different. What about tea then, Robert?'

'Well, Aunt, I'm already stuffed full with scones from the Bunts and I don't think I can manage anything just yet.'

'That's all right, we'll miss tea today and have a bit of supper later.'

The evening wore on and some cold supper was had off a tray in the lounge at about seven thirty. The curfew bell chimed slowly at 8 p.m. and the evening fell into that quietness which only a town such as Bodmin could generate.

'Well Robert, tomorrow we'll visit Leon and Alice out at Tall

Chimneys Farm, and I dare say we will see Anne and her brothers too.' She saw Robert's look. 'Well, she styles herself as Juliet now, doesn't she Robert,' and she smiled across at him.

Chapter Five

Robert awoke and was instantly aware that the long-awaited day of Thursday had arrived, with the visit to Juliet and her family arranged for later that day. The butterflies flooded back into his stomach again and rather than endure the anticipation, he leapt out of bed in an instant and was away to the bathroom without further ado.

Having washed, he returned to his room, dressed rapidly as quietly as possible, so as not to wake his aunt, glanced at his watch, ten to seven, that's early, he thought. He tiptoed to the door and continued tiptoeing downstairs in his bare feet. He entered the kitchen and lit the gas-stove burner by striking the flint lighter in the gas stream. He took the kettle to the tap over the sink and filled it about half-full. He placed the kettle on to the gas flame and, knowing that it would take a reasonably long time to boil, he sat down in the window alcove on the bench seat.

From here he could see directly across the road to Miss Mudge's farmhouse. It was stone-built with its surrounding wall topped by wooden railings painted a fading red, as was the front door. He pondered when it had last seen a lick of paint and what the interior of the house must be like. As far as he knew nobody had been in there, not even his aunt. It was far too early for Miss Mudge to take the cows up the hill; that wouldn't happen until much later in the morning. The only signs from the farmyard were the cock-a-doodle-dos from the few roosters kept there.

Dong, dong, dong... The church bell striking the hour of seven o'clock resonated to the back of the house. The kettle began to boil and he looked round for the teapot and caddy. The brown china teapot was easily found on the table, and he found the tea caddy in the cupboard by the sink. The cubed sugar bowl was on the table with the tongs sticking out from under the covering doily. He did not of course take sugar in his tea, only milk, and he retrieved the partially-full milk jug from the cool depths of the pantry across the hall. I have everything available to make a cup of tea now, he thought. I wonder if I ought to take one up to Aunt for a change? He thought better of it, thinking that she would probably not like to be disturbed in her own bedroom! Robert portioned out two spoonfuls of tea leaves into the pot, retrieved the kettle from the stove, holding the handle with a kitchen glove, and poured about two cups' worth of water into it. He left it to settle and to brew. He chose a large willow pattern cup from the dresser, poured in some milk and then some tea nearly to the top of the cup, and took a sip. Ah, that was good, he thought, his mouth was rather dry from the period spent in sleep. He sat in the wheel back armchair, sipped more tea and considered how the day's visit might work out.

He was looking out of the window for signs of the weather when he heard the characteristic sound of his aunt descending the stairs. She had to take them fairly steadily with her built-up shoe and there was the repeated sound of one step and then a clunk. It had been a great blow to her, the arthritis in her hip that had drawn the leg up. It had cut down her mobility, but she was a great sport and she and Robert's mother, when together, would often laugh at their respective conditions, saying what a couple of old crocks they were!

She opened the door and walked into the kitchen. She looked as fresh as a daisy in her silken dressing gown. Her skin was fair and her silver hair was hanging in two plaits over her shoulders prior to it being wound into a bun, as was her usual day fashion.

'Good morning my dear, down already?'

'Yes Aunt, I woke early this morning. Would you like a cup of tea? There is one in the pot.'

'Yes please, Robert, that would be wonderful.'

She sat down on her usual side of the table, the cooker side, and Robert poured her a cup and placed it before her. She stirred in one sugar cube and sipped. 'That's wonderful my dear, nothing like a good cup of tea first thing.'

Robert was pleased she liked it and realised that it was nice for her to be waited on for a change, although he had done very little really.

'We'll have breakfast fairly soon and then perhaps an early

light lunch and afterwards we'll be driving out to Tall Chimneys Farm. I said that we'd arrive about mid-afternoon, and we are invited to stay for high tea and supper. That should make a nice change,' she said.

Robert knew that nothing happened in a hurry down here and he would just have to abide with the time pattern. The country ways were a lot slower, particularly down in Bodmin!

Another giant breakfast was placed before him and he began to tuck in. He was feeling quite hungry by now. The church clock started to strike nine o'clock. That's the reason why I am hungry, thought Robert, I've been up since before seven and now it's nine!

'That was another fine breakfast, thank you, Aunt.'

'I'll go upstairs now and get dressed for the day,' said Hilda.

'Do you want me to clear away the breakfast things?' said Robert, anticipating the answer.

'No, no, my dear, you go and have a smoke and read the newspaper, I'll deal with the things when I come down.'

Oh well, thought Robert, I'll do what I'm told – no point arguing about it!

He went into the hall and to the front door; he picked up the paper from the doormat and took it into the lounge. He sat back in his favourite armchair, lit a cigarette and opened the paper. Pretty average stuff at this time of the year: the visitors who had poured into Cornwall during the holiday season, the rescues at sea, the farming economy and the general state of the duchy.

It seemed like an eternity before Aunt Hilda joined him in the lounge. It was just after eleven o'clock, as indicated by the church clock. Hilda said, 'We'll have a nice bowl of stew before we head out to Leon and Alice's. That will keep us in good stead until the evening. I've put some by and it will go down a treat with those crusty rolls I got from Jack Bray's yesterday.'

'That will be fine,' said Robert, 'it will certainly keep the wolf from the door until the evening!'

They sat chatting for a while on local events from the news, until Hilda stirred herself and made a move to the kitchen. 'I'll call you when it's ready, Robert.'

Robert stayed sitting and thought more about the visit. I'll be pleased when we are on the way, he thought to himself, all this hanging about is not good for one. I must get my own transport one day, he determined. I can't spend the rest of my life waiting on others, no matter how well-disposed they are. It's really only a short trip to the moor, and here we are treating it as a major journey. Robert did have a motorcycle once but had to get rid of it to help pay his way at university. He had no experience of driving cars. That would change on his return to London, he determined.

The stew was delicious and was followed with some more of the irresistible warmed-up apple pie with the clotted cream melting into every crevice of the pudding. Robert ate well again and considered that he would manage no more this day! The cup of tea afterwards had an even more bloating effect on him.

He staggered to the lounge and waited for his aunt to join him and to declare the afternoon trip on. She entered the lounge and Robert observed that she had dressed in a smart suit and had changed her shoes to best. Robert was in a checked shirt and khaki summer trousers with brown brogues and he carried a light sports jacket in case of inclement weather.

Hilda looked at Robert. 'Ready now my dear? We'll go across to Miss Mudge's to get the car.'

Robert's relief was palpable and showed in his enthusiasm to get going. The walk across was slow, as Robert had to keep pace with Hilda as she limped across the road.

They entered the farmyard entrance and encountered the outward flow of Miss Mudge's few cows on their way out to pasture. They stayed perfectly still on the edge of the path and tried to avoid the flicking tails on which was deposited a substantial portion of their slurry, something you wanted to avoid having flicked on to your clothes, particularly if you were going visiting! Miss Mudge followed her cows out. They knew where they were going and required very little guidance from her. She mumbled 'Hello Mrs Yudy, going to get the car?' She nodded to Robert. 'Enjoy your stay,' she said.

Robert nodded back and noticed how much more eccentric she seemed close up. Her long brown coat brushed the top of her wellington boots and her silver hair straggled out under her battered, verdigris-marked hat. Her jowls really hung low and the resemblance to her cows was clearer the closer you got. The cows moved on and Robert and Hilda reached the barn where Hilda kept her car. The few shillings of rent a week probably helped her more than they would know.

The barn door was opened and left open until the car's return. They got into the black Austin, Hilda in the driving seat and Robert in the front passenger seat. Hilda pulled out the choke and turned the key for the electric start. If that did not work, one would have to resort to the starting handle. That was something to be avoided! Mercifully, the engine turned over and with the appropriate amount of choke adjustment, pulled out of the barn and on to the hard standing. Hilda waited a while for the engine to warm up, then drove out to the farmyard gate and made a wide turn to the left up Castle Hill. She revved considerably and drove the car up the steep hill, past the doctor's, past the dentist's, past the camping site on the edge of the town and on to the edge of the moor. The road levelled out and the car picked up speed and purred along at forty miles per hour, a most appropriate speed for such a vehicle in this county.

Robert relaxed back into the leather seat and breathed a sigh of relief. It's nice to be on the move, he thought, and looked out at the stark beauty of the moor, the yellow-tipped gorse bushes, the sheets of water and the beckoning bleakness of the distant tors.

Suddenly, an AA motorcycle combination came round the bend in the road towards them and its driver gave them a snappy salute as he roared past. 'If I'm not mistaken, that was Mr Burton,' said Robert. 'I forgot to tell you Aunt, I saw him in town the other day and had a chat with him. He said he might call on you again next time he's in Bodmin.'

Her road concentration was fixed but she heard all that Robert said. 'Really? I have not seen him for a few years myself, but I would be most pleased to see him if he can call some time. He was an interesting character.'

'I think he is based in this area again now,' said Robert. The car moved on. Very few cars passed you on the other side of the road down here, thought Robert. It's quite an event when they do, and you certainly notice the whoosh. A combined collision speed of their individual velocities added together would be very large, thought Robert. He certainly did not hope for any such thing to happen, knowing the consequences of such! It was just science. He mused on. The momentum of any moving vehicle is directly proportional to the square of the velocity. Increase the speed, square it and you get an incredibly-increasing figure. It was all due to speed, he thought. His thoughts trailed away, avoiding the obvious conclusion. He went back to viewing the scenery.

The car swept past Racecourse Farm and Racecourse Down on the left where the point-to-points were held. His aunt observed that she knew the people there as well. They drove on past the sign to Cardingham and Cardingham Down on the right and on towards Temple. At the road junction with the sign pointing right to Temple, Hilda swung the car left off the main road with her very definite action of feeding the black, ribbed steering wheel correctly through her hands and on in the direction of St Breward. She turned the car left in her characteristic manner at the signpost to Treswigga and down to the left to Metherin and into the gravelled courtyard entrance of Mentreaths Farm. She swung the car to the right, its tyres crunching satisfyingly across the gravel as she brought it to a rest in front of the porticoed Entrance. The two granite columns forming the portico were of the Palladian architecture style and were most pleasing to Robert's eye. The farmhouse building, at least from the front, seemed to be of a Georgian style. However, Robert knew it could have much older origins, with the front piece being a later addition.

'Well, here we are my dear,' said Hilda as she struggled out of the driving seat. Robert stepped out on to the gravel pensively. They walked to the front door, which was ajar, and Hilda cooeed into the hall. 'Hello Alice, anybody there? We've arrived.'

All was still – there was no answer. They waited for a few minutes, then Hilda said, 'She is probably out the back, we'll go on through.'

They walked through the gloom of the long hall, past doors to reception rooms on the left and right, and entered a flagstoned kitchen, where a well-built woman was bending over a coal fire range, attending to scones it would seem. Startled, she turned. 'My goodness Hilda, is it you? You fair startled me. Lovely to see you my dear, after all this time!' She moved to Hilda, wiping her hands on her apron, and embraced her.

'Alice, so good to see you again, 'howvy been keeping?'

'Fine, my dear, plenty to do. Have not been to town for some time, as you know. Leon, the boys and Anne are out on the combine, harvesting the top two fields. Those fields are being harvested early this year due to the fine weather and the hay will make up the cattle feed.'

When Robert heard the name Anne, a bolt shot through his heart. Heavens, that's Juliet, he thought, I dare say that I will be seeing her soon.

Alice turned to him. 'This must be Robert,' she said. 'My, how you have grown since I last saw you, and doing so well too.'

'Nice to see you again Alice, it's lovely to be down here again,' said Robert.

''Ess,' she replied, ''specially now it's such good weather. Well my dears, I was just doing a few scones for teatime and they are just about ready.' She turned to the range, opened the door, took out three trays of scones and placed them out to rest on the kitchen table. 'I'll leave them there to cool,' said Alice, 'and we'll go through to the parlour for a chat.'

She led the way, and Hilda and Robert followed. They walked past the dining room and entered the parlour, which was on the sunniest side of the house. The sun streamed through the window and deeply into the room, brightening up the heavy brocade curtains at the window and the draught-excluding curtain hanging from the rail behind the door. They sat in three comfortable wingback chairs arranged around the fireplace, with the remains of last night's log fire still on show in the grate. The brass coal scuttle was piled high with logs, and some had spilled out on to the hearth. The room was warm enough at the moment without needing a fire.

Hilda and Alice chatted on, catching up on past events and histories, and Robert was fairly silent except when asked a direct question, to which he responded the best way he could, being somewhat distracted by thinking about the arrival of Juliet all the time.

The grandfather clock chimed four in the hall and Alice remarked, 'How time flies,' and hurried to bring in tea and scones, strawberry jam and cream and Cornish splits. They ate up well and drank plenty of tea. 'You'll stay on for supper later on. Leon, the boys and Anne will be in later for supper and we can have a nice get-together with them then.'

Hilda accepted and Robert breathed an inward deep sigh of relief. That was touch and go, he thought. He was beginning to think that they would have to go back without seeing them, and by 'them', he really meant Juliet.

Chapter Six

Alice went off to busy herself getting the supper together and burdening the large table in the dining room with it all. Hilda and Robert sat on for a while, talking, and then Hilda departed to give Alice a hand in the kitchen and to assist in loading the supper table. Robert remained, looking around the room at the various pieces of furniture. Many were family heirlooms and hand-me-downs and he noticed the oil lamps. They were still not on electricity up here then, and had to rely on oil lamps for their night-time lighting. He remembered as an excited young lad, being allowed to wander round the farmyard area and fields taking in all the interesting aspects of farming. Leon allowed him to wander round with an old .22 bolt action rifle – no ammunition of course – and Robert would pretend he was shooting vermin and the like, vigorously cocking and firing the mechanism as often as possible. Robert wondered now whether or not it was still a viable rifle after all his misuse of it!

He sat quietly in the room, just hearing the Cornish brogues of Alice and Hilda as their voices filtered through when they were going to and fro between the kitchen and the dining room. From a distance, the Cornish brogue often sounded almost American, with its rolled R's and quaint expressions. I expect, he thought, that the original English country accents had contributed largely in the formation of the American accent, very removed from the establishment's 'acceptable' Oxford accent of the BBC!

Robert's ears pricked up as he heard new voices from the back of the house. My word, they are back from the haymaking now, and his heart raced a little faster than usual. He grabbed for a cigarette but though better of it. Perhaps they did not like smoking in the parlour.

The door swung open and in strode Leon, every inch a farmer, from his steel-shod brown boots and gaiters, his strong twill trousers, leather belt, waistcoat with watch chain, and his collarless shirt to his thin moustache and his sandy but greying hair on top. He threw his cloth cap into the far chair and said, 'Is it Robert then? I have not seen you for a few years boy – my, you've grown.'

Robert stood up and gripped Leon's hand. It was a firm handshake. Leon had an iron grip and Robert noticed the strength of his wrist and forearm. Farming undoubtedly made you strong, reflected Robert, unlike us desk wallahs! They both sat down and got into discussion on farming, agricultural engineering and electricity supply to remote areas. 'You sound like you ought to be getting involved in electricity supply to remote areas,' said Leon to Robert, 'with your background, plenty of scope for that down here.'

Robert replied that he would not mind, but it was the luck of the draw where you ended up. However, he'd be keen on the idea if the opportunity came along.

The door opened and the three sons walked in: James, Giles and John. They were massively built, no doubt due to the heavy work they did, farming and repairing of tractors etc, but undoubtedly the feeding up from their mother had contributed greatly to their size also. They were shy giants and came forward to shake his hand one by one. They had massive hands like great plates of meat, but their grips were gentler than their father's. They had really spent most of their lives immersed on the farm that no doubt had contributed to their quiet shyness. They were, however, extremely hospitable and welcoming to guests and remembered Robert from his younger days. Robert felt a little out of place with them at first, as his lifestyle was so different to theirs, but they warmed to one another as they talked on, having much more in common than first realised.

The door swung open and in walked Hilda, Alice and Juliet. Robert's heart jumped.

'Well, how are you boys getting on, then?' said Hilda.

'Fine,' responded Leon. 'We've been getting on like a house on fire. Robert's a fine chap and we may have persuaded him to take up the farming life with us down at Tall Chimneys.'

Robert grinned and nodded in assent to this, and turned his

gaze to Juliet. She looked different to how he had last seen her. She was wearing corduroy trousers, wellington boots and a loose, checked shirt that could have been one of her brother's. Her hair was pulled back, but strands were spilling out of the hair band. Well, she is every inch the farming girl, thought Robert, particularly when she has been helping with the haymaking. He found this aspect of her equally as attractive as the day-dressed girl he had met on the train. He walked over to where the ladies were standing and Alice said, 'I believe you two have already met up previously,' glancing across at Hilda.

'Yes, we have, and I am very pleased to meet again,' said Robert, grasping Juliet's hand. They both grinned at one another and spluttered a few words of greeting. 'It's lovely to see you again, Juliet.'

'And you too, Robert,' she responded.

'Why don't you two young people sit over there on the settee,' said Alice. 'Hilda, you come with me to the kitchen, and Leon, boys, you better get washed up for your supper.'

They all dutifully responded to Alice's request and Robert and Juliet were left alone in the parlour to renew the acquaintance of their first meeting on the train.

'It's good to se you again Juliet, wherever did you get to at the station?' blurted out Robert.

'Oh Robert, I'm so sorry about that, I did not intend to disappear like that,' she responded. 'What happened was that Giles had come down to pick me up from Bodmin Road, and just could not wait as they had a crisis up here on the farm. One of the cows had got stuck in some deep mud on the edge of the moor and had fallen, and he had to collect some lifting gear from Halgavor farm on the other side of Bodmin, and on the way he collected me. It was all a mad rush to save the cow, but it was successful in the end. I did think that we would meet up again anyhow,' she said. 'I did not know of course that you were Auntie's nephew Robert at the time. We had not seen one another since we were children, had we?'

'No,' said Robert, remembering now that Juliet had referred to his aunt as 'Auntie' due to the long-standing relationship between them. Robert's visits to his aunt in latter years had never seemed to coincide with the presence of Juliet! Robert mentioned this to her and she thought it was strange too. It was a pity they had not met up a bit more often in the past. 'Still, we're meeting up now aren't we,' said Robert, 'and that's the important thing, isn't it?'

Juliet nodded in assent.

'I do remember going to the seaside with you in Aunt's car at least once,' said Robert. 'I think it was Mevagissy or was it Parr sands?'

'I think I remember going too,' said Juliet. 'It was an exciting trip, with a picnic basket on the beach and the fishermen hauling their nets up on the beach with lots of fish in them.'

'Yes, I think that was the one,' he responded, 'I do remember the fishermen!'

Their conversation continued, she with the recent events on the farm and he relating his visits in town. He made her laugh when he related the idiosyncrasies of Mrs Sandow and the Bunts, and she agreed, as she had often met them down at the church on Sundays, but they seemed to be getting worse from his account. They had much in common, similar interests and similar values, and a deeper bond was already growing between them.

The clock chimed six thirty in the hall. 'Is that the time?' said Juliet. 'Well, I must go and tidy myself up for supper before it's too late.' She jumped up from the settee and moved towards the door. Turning, she smiled back at Robert, saying, 'See you at supper, Robert.'

Robert sat on, feeling very content with all that had transpired, and that he and Juliet were now reunited.

'Robert, Robert.' His contented silence was broken by Hilda's call. 'Supper is now ready in the dining room – come on through now, my dear.'

He went through the parlour door into the gloom of the hall, along and into the dining room. What met him was a magnificently laid table, groaning under the weight of a cornucopia of produce, illuminated by the warming light from two table oil lamps. The evening had moved on, throwing its lengthening shadows and by now the illumination was necessary. Leon was at the head of the table with Alice at his right hand and John the elder at his left hand. Hilda sat next to Alice and then James the middle boy and Giles the younger at the bottom end of the table. Two places were vacant. Robert sat next to Giles and the only remaining seat was left vacant for Juliet, the youngest, between Robert and John.

'Anne's not down yet,' said Alice, 'but I think we'll start anyway, she won't mind. It's getting on and you know what they say about going to bed on a full stomach, you'll be getting nightmares.'

'Couldn't 'ave been a worse nightmare than with that cow stuck in the mud the other day,' piped up Leon, 'and I hadn't been eatin' too much then, m'dear.'

They all had a good laugh at Leon's outburst and Alice said, 'Get on with it then, eat up, good people!'

Great dining plates were then loaded with sliced, home-cooked ham, meat patties, boiled potatoes, beetroot and home-grown tomatoes, and passed around the table and everybody tucked in. Juliet slipped into the room and Robert glanced at her as she quietly took her place next to him at the table. She looked transformed from previously. She was wearing a dress, her hair was down and combed, and her silver earrings matching her wristband as they glistened in the flickering light of the oil lamps. Wow, she does look glamorous, thought Robert. As if to echo his thoughts, Hilda said, 'Well my dear, you are looking very pretty.'

'Thank you, Auntie,' she said.

'What will you be eating, my dear?' exclaimed Alice over the general conversational hubbub of the table.

'I'll just have a small piece of Pasty, thank you, Mother,' she replied. Robert had been heavily engaged in conversation with Giles to his left, and now found it difficult to break off to converse with Juliet. He did however manage it in fits and starts, and managed to say how beautiful she looked in her dress and earrings, and that perhaps they could meet up on their own sometime whilst he was staying with his aunt. Juliet was happy to agree to this and thought that it would be nice if they could have an uninterrupted evening together, and it was just a question of when.

The dessert was an enormous sherry trifle topped with lashings of clotted cream. After they had all eaten their fill, Alice said,

'You'll all have coffee now, my dears. Come on ladies, we'll go and prepare this. You give me a hand Hilda, and Anne, can you get the best coffee cups and spoons from the sideboard? The menfolk, go and sit yourselves down in the parlour.'

Alice was immediately obeyed and the men dutifully departed to the parlour, seated themselves and lit up pipes and cigarettes.

The ladies brought the coffee through, sat amongst the men and the conversation continued well on into the evening. Robert and Juliet managed to exchange as much conversation as they could under the circumstances of the general conversational melee and Robert managed to suggest to Juliet that they meet up on Saturday evening and go to a nearby pub for a drink. Juliet was very happy with this, as Saturday evening was generally a free evening for her, and of course she would be only too happy to meet him alone!

The evening drew to its conclusion. 'Well, my dears all, Robert and I must be departing. It's getting late now and Bodmint has drawn her curfew. We'll be very lucky to get back into town again after being out here so long.'

They all laughed at this reference to the town's curfew – it was a standing joke that if you did not get back into town before the eight o'clock curfew bell, then they would not let you back in again until the morning!

'It's been a lovely evening Alice and Leon, and boys and Anne, thank you so much.' Robert reiterated Hilda's thanks and they moved towards the front door portico.

'It's been good to see you again, Hilda and Robert. Don't leave it so long next time, maid,' said Leon. 'Although we should get down again more regular to St Petroc's 'fore too long at the end of the harvest, so hope to see more of you then.'

'Come in for tea when you're down,' said Hilda.

They shook hands and kissed cheeks all round, and then Robert was in front of Juliet under the star-laden sky. He wanted to embrace her and take her fully in his arms, but under the circumstances he held back. He clasped her hands and said, 'I'll call Saturday night then, at seven thirty, hope that's OK.'

'Yes Robert, that will be lovely, I'm really looking forward to it. Bye for now.'

Robert and Hilda got into the car. It started on electric but heavily choked. The evening was colder now. They pulled out of the drive and Robert turned to wave. The family stood on the portico step, illuminated by the porch lamp, and waved them off. The car turned right into the lane and Robert saw Juliet was the last to turn indoors. The car pulled up the dark narrow road on the way back. Hilda revved furiously to enable the car to climb up the hill, and then they were on their way back to the old town of Bodmin.

Chapter Seven

Robert awoke. It was Friday. The recollections of yesterday's events flooded back into his mind. The visit and the meeting with Juliet and her family had passed very smoothly and more perfectly, they had arranged to meet again on Saturday evening! It had gone very well, although the fuller communication he had anticipated with her had been somewhat curtailed under the circumstances of meeting her directly within the bosom of her family. Not that he found Alice, Leon and the boys difficult company – on the contrary, they were delightful people and most interesting. However, his focus on Juliet was modified by their presence. Now he had the opportunity to meet her on her own. That was food for thought. He wondered how it would work out on Saturday, and lay back and luxuriated in contented anticipation of the meeting. He had slept on later this morning and had not time as he had yesterday to get out of bed before the arrival of Hilda with the tea tray.

Hilda walked in. 'Morning my dear, did you sleep well?'

'Like a log, Aunt, it must have been all the excitement of yesterday. It took its toll but I slept content.'

'Yes, I did too my dear. I really enjoyed the visit, a bit of an event for me these days. They are lovely people. I've known Leon and Alice all the years I've lived here, and I've seen the growing up of their boys and Anne over the years. You seemed to be getting on with Anne like a house on fire my dear, or perhaps now I should call her Juliet,' she said, recognising that Robert's relationship with her seemed to be conducted with her solely on the use of her third Christian name. Well, thought Hilda, 'lucky number three, holy trinity, all will be well with thee', quoting to herself a little devotional ditty she had learnt at Sunday school all those years ago.

'Yes Aunt, I can't really see her as an Anne now but only as a Juliet, I'm afraid.'

'Well my dear, Juliet is a lovely name and it certainly has a ring to it. It does make Anne seem a bit dull by comparison, I must say!' Hilda turned to leave the room saying, 'Breakfast will be ready when you're down, my dear. See you soon, but don't hurry on my account, we don't have to rush anywhere today.'

Robert cracked the biscuits and drank the tea. Yes, he thought, Juliet does have a certain resonance to it. I suppose that's probably why Shakespeare chose it for the character in *Romeo and Juliet*. Not that Robert was claiming any affinity with the Romeo character, whom he thought was a somewhat frivolous individual, unlike himself!

Robert descended for breakfast. His aunt was in full fray and turned out a mighty breakfast for him again. Robert was getting used to this by now and was beginning to expect it.

Hilda interrupted his thoughts. 'You know that letter I got from Aunt Aggie the other day? Well, she did say she would like you to stay with her for a few days at Porth, so I thought it might be a good idea to go down on Sunday after lunch.'

'That would be fine, Aunt,' said Robert, thinking that the reunion with his cousins would be grand.

'What are you doing today, my dear? You seem to have done all the visiting around Bodmin for a bit.'

'I don't know exactly, Aunt, other than pop downtown for another mooch around. I might even have a walk up to the beacon or down to the river.'

'I've got to go to an extraordinary Conservatives meeting this morning at the town hall offices, but I thought that this afternoon we might pop down to Respryn for a bit of a picnic and you might cast a line in the river for a while.'

'I'd like that, Aunt. While I'm downtown I'll call in at the tackle shop and get a licence.'

'That's settled then,' said Hilda. 'I'll meet you back here about midday and we'll go to Respryn this afternoon. I'll take some pasties and thermos flasks for tea.'

Hilda left the house before Robert today and limped off determinedly down the garden path to do battle at the town hall offices. Robert knew that she was chairwoman of the local executive committee, and that she did not budge an inch on matters of principal, especially when it came to the Church of England, the Conservative party, the royal family or the country. The local Liberal candidate, Dingle Foot, was her arch-enemy as she despised any leanings to liberalism, particularly anything to do with actual socialism. Robert knew well enough not to argue or cross her on any of her matters of principal, as it was far better to have a relaxing time with her rather than one of conflict.

Saturday night was the main event on his mind at the moment but the problem was, how would he get over there? There was no bus service in that direction at night and he did not want to have to rely on his aunt for transport there and to pick him up as well. A taxi would do it, but it would be very expensive for the pick-up at night. He dismissed the issue, again, from his mind for the moment, but he knew that the concern of it would drift back in sooner or later.

He looked out of the lounge window and just saw Hilda disappearing down the road. Robert lit up a cigarette and inhaled the smoke. He felt the stimulus of the nicotine surge through his bloodstream, became rather giddy and sat down in his favourite chair. He did not like it when the cigarettes caused this sensation and waited for the moment to pass. Once it had he gathered himself together for his sojourn into town that morning.

Robert walked downtown past St Petroc's, noticing that the water from the spring outlet was still in full flow and was gurgling away in the trough below before finally rushing away to the drain beneath. It's amazing, he thought, how much water there is available. He had never known this spring to run dry, although he supposed in dryer weather its flow undoubtedly reduced.

Robert crossed over into Honey Street and headed for the fishing tackle shop. He entered and browsed around as he had done the day previously. The magnificent split cane rods and the centre pin reels were still there and he briefly looked them over, thinking that one day he would be buying such a set! He browsed further around the shop, looking at the array of floats and fishing line that you could get these days. The old cat-gut was a thing of the past, and modern nylon lines were all the rage – unless you were a fly purist of course. A whole range of breaking strains were to be had from the heavy 30–40 lb sea line down to the 3–5 lb light line one used for river fishing. Light tackle was the key if you wanted your trout fishing to be sporting!

Robert detected movement from behind the counter and looked up to see the proprietor of the shop whom he had spoken to previously.

'Morning, sir, can I help you?' said the proprietor in his distinctive Cornish burr.

'Hello again,' said Robert, 'I'm back. Got a bit of fishing planned for down at Respryn this afternoon, and I will need a river-board licence. You will have to remind me how much they are.' With all the activities since his last visit here, Robert had forgotten the prices quoted to him previously.

'Five pounds for the season or ten shillings for a fortnight,' came the reply.

'Oh yes, I remember now, you quoted that to me before. As I am only here for a short time, I'll take the fortnight one please.'

The proprietor got out the permit book, asked Robert his name and address, filled in the details and said, 'Sign here please, Sir, and that will be ten shillings.'

Robert reached into his jacket inside pocket for his leather wallet and removed a ten shilling note and handed it over to the proprietor, who in exchange handed Robert the fishing permit.

'Thank you sir, would you like any tackle to use at Respryn?'

'Well, I've got all the basics,' said Robert. 'I brought my light rod, reel and line down with me in anticipation, but I will need some bait. Do you have any brandling worms in at the moment?'

'I've got plenty of 'em sir. In fact, I've got me own little factory of 'em out back.'

The proprietor walked out to the back and returned with a small cardboard box full of worms. 'There you are sir, the best sixpence' worth of worms in the county!'

Robert dug into his trouser pocket, rattled the change around and found a sixpenny piece to give to the proprietor.

'Thank you sir, have a good afternoon's fishing. Remember to 'return' your catch on the back of the licence and send it off to the river board when you can.'

Robert walked out of the shop and wondered what he would do to kill a bit of time before meeting his aunt at midday. I know, he thought, I'll walk up to the beacon, I have not been up there for a long time and it's a good view from there. The beacon, on a steep, windswept hill just above the town, was a 144-foot obelisk erected in memory of Sir Walter Raleigh Gilbert, a descendent of the famous English sailor, commemorating his distinguished service in India.

Robert walked on up Honey Street past Jack Bray's and turned left into Fore Street, past the town hall and then right into St Nicholas Street, past the Post office and immediately right up towards the beacon. The hill was steeping considerably as he progressed and he began to feel the strain in his breathing. Heavens thought Robert the 'old steel band round the chest again', I'm pretty unfit, and the smoking is certainly not helping!

He progressed on and eventually arrived at the base of the beacon. By now he had got his second wind and was feeling a lot better. He read the inscription at the base, reminding him for whom the beacon was erected, and thought that it must have cost a pretty penny at the time and wondered if the recipient of the honour was really worthy of such a memorial. He turned his gaze away from the beacon and looked out to the magnificent view over the town and to the hills beyond. It was worth the haul up here, he thought, if only for this view. He retraced his steps back down the hill and down St Nicholas Street. He decided to cut back through Priory Park, across Priory Road and stopped at the granite wall of the police station. He had been brought here many times by his mother and his aunt as a young boy, to look at the tortoise that was kept in the garden grounds. To him, at that age, it appeared to be enormous. Observing it now, it was only of moderate size, but had been there for many years and it was certainly a tradition!

He walked on up Pound Lane and left into Castle Street and down to his aunt's house in Castle Hill. He opened the garden gate just as the church clock chimed a quarter to twelve. He walked into the house and called out. There was no reply – his aunt had obviously not yet returned from her meeting. Robert went into the lounge, sat down and lit up a cigarette.

A short time later Hilda walked into the house and cooeed for Robert.

'I'm in the lounge,' shouted Robert, and Hilda limped in, finding him deeply engrossed in The *Western Morning News*.

That's probably why he did not notice me coming up the garden path, she thought.

'How did the meeting go, Aunt?' said Robert.

'It was a load of old stuff and nonsense,' she said. 'They only want to widen Priory Road and in the process knock down the two monks' cells next to the road in the park that have been there for centuries! They'll do that over my dead body!'

Robert mumbled a non-committal reply to the effect that it would be a shame to lose them. Hilda went on, 'I'd be getting on to Viscount Vivian over this. I'm sure he won't be wanting to lose such historical pieces as these. They belong to the town.'

Viscount Vivian was in fact of that different political persuasion so abhorrent to Hilda. However, in such an emergency, she was prepared to recruit such an advocate – after all, he did have the interests of Bodmin at heart before party politicking! Robert did think that all this was rather ironic, as Hilda, a great advocate for the Church of England, would have unwittingly supported the king that dissolved the monasteries in the first place, and that was why they had only a few of the ruins left – and now they were desperate to preserve them!

'How did you get on then, Robert?'

'I went to the tackle shop and got a river-board licence to cover me for while I'm down here, and managed to get a box of brandling worms.'

'He's keeping worms now, is he?' replied Hilda. 'That's good, nothing like a few brandlings to attract the trout. Good you managed to get a lot of 'em, nothing worse than running short when the trout are biting. If Uncle Percy and I ran short on occasion, there was nothing for it but to crack a cowpat or two open to find one,' and she chuckled at the memory. 'Well my dear, I'll warm up some pasties for us for lunch and then we'll pop down to Respryn for a bit of afternoon fishing.'

After lunch, they walked slowly across to Miss Mudge's to get the car. Robert was carrying the picnic basket. Hilda drove the car out of the barn and halted, and Robert loaded the picnic basket into the boot. He slipped into the front passenger seat and sat back against the warmth of the leather. Hilda clonked the car into first gear and they moved slowly forward to turn right down Castle Hill. She activated the right-hand indicator and the little yellow arm flicked out in response. They motored carefully down the hill past St Petroc's on the left and across the road junction up to St Nicholas Street, past Bodmin Town station, past the DCLI Barracks and on to the Lostwithiel road or 'Lost with all' as the name of the town was colloquially pronounced. The car picked up speed and Hilda changed up the gears, and they were on the road to Respryn.

On reaching Trebyan they diverted left and followed the road all the way to the River Fowey flowing under the old bridge at Respryn. Hilda parked the car in a small lay-by just before the bridge. The bridge itself was very narrow and could only be traversed by one car at a time. It was granite built, very solid and had pedestrian ports either side where pedestrians could stand back from any cars going over the bridge. Not that there was much traffic over this bridge in such a quiet area. The railway line ran down from Bodmin Road in the Fowey river valley to Lostwithiel and on to St Austell. It ran in reasonable proximity to the river but the trains were few and far between, and hardly a disturbance.

Hilda said, 'You go on and do your fishing now my dear. Auntie will sit here and when you come back, we'll have our picnic down by the river, this side.'

Robert took her at her word, picked up the tackle and the box of worms from the rear of the car, walked over the bridge and ducked left under the perimeter wire of the farmer's field on the way to his favourite fishing spot. He walked across the field, carefully avoiding the cud-chewing cows that were occasionally eying him suspiciously when they raised their heads from their business of cropping grass. He walked down to the river and along the bank for a few hundred yards to a particular bend that had always served him well in the past with its harvest of fish. He sat down on the sandy bank with his feet resting in the dry culvert at the river's edge. He assembled his whippy cane rod, fixed on the centre pin reel and threaded the light line through the rings. He selected one of the smaller hooks, tied it on to the line and weighted the line with enough split shot just to achieve a decent cast. He baited up the hook with two or three brandling worms, pulled some line off the reel and cast it across towards the opposite bank into a deep pool which he suspected of harbouring trout. Thankfully, he avoided becoming snagged in the branches of the overhanging trees. He reeled back the spare line, held it between his forefinger and thumb, keeping the line taut in the direction of the pool. He leaned back against the bank, waiting and relaxing in the warm sun. He was serene and thoughts of Juliet flooded back into his mind. It's wonderful, he thought, that tomorrow evening, Saturday, I will be meeting with Juliet again!

His thoughts were interrupted by an urgent tug, tugging on the line. My word, a bite! Hold for a moment, he instructed himself, let the bite develop but don't leave it too late. He struck slowly, tightening back on the line gradually. Yes, it was firm; there was definitely a fish on it. The rod bent over as the fish dived off to try to hide away in the weeds. He reeled for a tighter line and raised the tip of the rod to keep the fish up in play. It was exciting – the fish was darting in all directions endeavouring to get off the hook, but it was tiring itself. Robert gradually reeled it in towards the bank and beached it.

He held the trout in his left hand, covering the gills. It was a clean hook through the lip and with his right hand he worked the hook out easily. It was a good fish – about a pound in weight and Robert dispatched it with a sharp crack to the head on a nearby boulder. It was a beautiful, speckled, brown trout, as good as any he had previously caught or seen in illustrations. He laid it in the fishing bag he kept for his catch. He felt at one with nature and a contentment came upon him with the realisation that impinged upon him from time to time that creation did exist!

Robert carried on fishing and caught another five fish that afternoon with a couple of missed ones and the odd line snarl-up. An express thundered by on the nearby line, steam and smoke belching out above the tree line. Its whistle was shrill and put Robert's nerves on edge as it thundered on to Lostwithiel. Robert looked at his watch – four o'clock already. I'd better pack up now and get back to Aunt, otherwise she's going to be feeling a little put out if I'm too long down here, he thought.

He broke down his rod, packed away the tackle, and picked up the tackle bag in one hand and the catch bag in the other and wandered back to the car. Nearing it, he noticed that his aunt had nodded off, and he wondered how long she had been snoozing. She awoke with a start when he opened the car door. 'Whateverisit?' she blurted out. She collected herself, recognised Robert and said, 'How did you get on, my dear?'

Robert showed her the catch.

'That's lovely my dear, all about a pound each. That's a good catch for here at this time of the year. I'll fry them up for supper for you tonight.'

'Thanks, Aunt,' said Robert.

He got the picnic hamper out of the car boot and carried it down to the riverbank. He went back to collect the picnic table and chairs, set them up and finally returned to Hilda and helped her down the bank on his arm. Hilda occasionally had to concede that she could not do everything, particularly when it came to getting down steep banks with that leg of hers. They sat down and Hilda got out the pasties, plates and knives, and poured the hot water from the flask onto the tea leaves in the teapot. They drank the refreshing cups of tea and ate the cold pasties.

'It's sure enough a beautiful spot down here,' said Hilda, 'You can't beat it.'

Their conversation waxed and waned softly, and when there was nothing left to say, they went quiet with their own thoughts and listened to the babbling sounds of the river as it flowed close by.

They returned to Bodmin the way they had come in the early evening and Hilda did the promised fry-up of the trout, the catch of the day, and they tasted as sweet as a nut!

Chapter Eight

It was Saturday. Robert was up early, far earlier than usual. His aunt was still in bed and Robert did not want to disturb her. He had made himself a cup of tea and was seated in the armchair in the kitchen drinking it. He was thinking about his meeting with Juliet tonight. He was certainly a bit nervous, as they had not intentionally been alone together before. Nevertheless, he was sure it would go well, the only problem being in what manner was he to get out there to meet her, take her out, and return her to Tall Chimneys and return home himself. There's no other way, he concluded, I will just have to go to town this morning, call in at the taxi firm's offices and book a cab to cover us for the whole evening. It would be expensive, thought Robert, keeping a cab on standby all evening, but there was no other way around it under the circumstances.

He had made up his mind on the matter then, but how to broach it to his aunt was another matter. She would undoubtedly offer her services with the car and this would really upset the whole intention of a private evening as far as Robert was concerned. He took his mind off it for a while and thought about what pub to go to that evening. He did not have a clue as to what the pubs were like out around the moor and did not want to bring her all the way back into town to go to the Hole in the Wall, for instance, as it was an old boys' pub and not really suitable for young women.

He idly thumbed through his aunt's AA membership book of the area which he had picked up from the window bench seat. The last few pages covered visitor attractions in the area for those fortunate enough with cars to go and visit. He flicked through the pages and them his eye alighted on one name – 'Jamaica Inn' – at Bolventor. Heavens, that was just down the road from Tall Chimneys, and Jamaica Inn, well, that was famous what with all the connotations with the smuggling that went on there in the past. What a fool he was not to have thought about that before! It was also close to Dozmary Pool, he noticed. That's worth a look at sometime whilst I'm down here, he thought. He remembered being there a few years ago, with its atmospheric association with the King Arthur story. He just had to wait now for the shops in town to open before going down there to organise the transport.

He heard Hilda moving upstairs and rapidly refilled the kettle and put it on the stove to boil up for more tea for her. He heard her descending the stairs in her characteristic manner and then she entered the kitchen. 'Good morning my dear, you're up early again.'

'Yes, Aunt,' he replied, 'I slept like a log again and feel well rested, it must have been the good air at Respryn yesterday.'

''Ess, it's a lovely spot down there, very restful, and it does wonders for your constitution.'

The kettle boiled and Robert moved to make up a pot of tea. Hilda endeavoured to take over this task but Robert insisted and Hilda was pleased in the end to have a cup of tea made for her. She said that there was nothing like a good cup of tea first thing in the morning and Robert agreed. 'That was lovely my dear, and now I'll be getting the breakfast on. You go and get ready for the day now.'

Robert, still in his dressing gown, thought that was a good idea and bounded off up the stairs to wash and change, leaving Hilda to take charge of her kitchen domain.

On his return he entered a smoky kitchen. Hilda had battled away at the breakfast and it was ready in his place: sausages, eggs, bacon and toast. 'No hogs pudding today Robert, I'm afraid, but the sausages are made locally by my butcher and are very good.'

Robert got stuck into the breakfast and the sausages were really very tasty. 'I must take a few of these home for mother when I go back to London,' he said. 'Do you think they will keep?'

'Well, they will for a few days, my dear, providing you keep them in a cool place. The spices in them should keep them for a while.' Then came the inevitable question. 'What are you going to do today, my dear? Tomorrow we're going down to Porth, so I would rest up for a bit if I was you.'

'Well, Aunt, I'll pop down to town for a bit [Robert knowing that he was going to organise a taxi for this evening], can I get you anything whilst I am down there?' Then he blurted it out, 'I've arranged to go over to Tall Chimneys this evening to meet up with Juliet.'

'Oh, that will be nice for both of you. You are both single and young, and you don't want to be stuck around us old fogies all the time, do you.'

Robert was pleased with this benign reaction from her. Then it came. 'But, my dear, how will you ever get over there and back?'

Silence reigned for a few moments, seeming like an eternity. 'I'll take you over myself and bring you back when you're ready.'

'That's lovely of you to offer, Aunt, but I don't want to trouble you, and I can go and organise a taxi.'

'Well, if you use Brewer's Taxis then, it will cost you a pretty penny.'

'Yes Aunt,' Robert responded, 'but I'm taking her out to Jamaica Inn and it will be too late for you to pick us up, and I know that you don't like driving after dark on these unlit roads, do you?'

'That's true, my dear, but I would not want you to go to such expense if it could be avoided.' The argument went to and fro until Hilda conceded the point that Robert was determined to go independently and, as she admitted to herself, she did not care too much for late-night driving, as she knew her vision at night was not as good as it was during daylight hours.

That was settled then, much to the relief of Robert, and all he had to do now was to go to town and make arrangements for booking the taxi. Breakfast over, Hilda cleared away and was going to busy herself with a few household chores that morning. Robert retired to the lounge for his usual first smoke of the day. He puffed away, looking out of the window. It was another fine August day and should be a fine evening. However, down here the weather was quite variable being a peninsular. On one coast it would be fine and on the other it would be wet and that would change about later in the day depending on the prevailing winds and the clouds.

The general weather did not particularly concern him at the moment; he only hoped that it would remain fine for the evening. Robert crushed out his cigarette and walked into the hall towards the front door. He had left his fishing rod in the hallstand from yesterday and noticed it as he passed. The remaining brandling worms he had discarded on the riverbank, knowing that they would not keep too long in their captive condition.

Robert walked on down to town, following the usual route. Arriving at the steps to St Petroc's, he crossed over to Honey Street on his way to find Brewer's Taxis, situated in a small road higher up off Fore Street.

Crossing over, he noticed an AA motorcycle parked up in front of the fishing tackle shop, and remarkably a patrolman was leaning against the bike smoking a cigarette. That can't be Mr Burton again, can it? thought Robert. His question was soon answered when he drew near and recognised that it was indeed Mr Burton.

'Hello again Mr Burton, you're back again, so soon.'

'Hello boy, yes I am, I'm afraid, I am. I've been told to patrol this area more often, particularly now that we're getting more visitors to the area. Just stopped off for me fag break,' he said, grinning at Robert.

'My aunt and I were driving out on the moor on Thursday afternoon towards Bolventor, and a patrolman passed us and saluted, and I'm sure that it was you.'

Mr Burton thought for a moment. 'Was it an Austin?' he said.

'Yes,' said Robert.

'Yes, it was me then. I was returning from that way about that time. Your aunt still driving then, is she?'

Robert replied in the affirmative and Mr Burton said 'good for her at her age too! What were you doing over that way, then?' he went on.

Robert explained the purpose of the visit and his growing friendship with Juliet.

'Nothing like it boy, get a good woman behind thee,' Mr Burton said enthusiastically.

Robert had not quite thought of their friendship under those terms, at least not yet, and went on to explain his meeting again with Juliet this evening.

'Your aunt taking you out there then, is she?'

'Well, no,' and Robert went on to explain that he was on his way to book a taxi for the evening.

'They're a bit expensive,' said Mr Burton, as he pondered the point. 'I tell 'ee what, boy, I've got an offer for you.' Robert looked interested, waiting to hear the details of the offer.

'I've got an old motorbike back at the depot at Liskeard, which you are welcome to borrow. I think it still works. It's an old BSA Gold, single cylinder, 500 cc, four-stroke, and it goes a treat when it's running. What do you think?'

Robert responded with a tentative, drawn-out 'Y-e-es,' thinking, Well, it would certainly save money. He did still have his two wheeled vehicle licence, but what would Juliet think, and could she ride pillion? 'Yes, Mr Burton, that's a very fine offer, but what about insurance and how do I get the bike?' Liskeard was about fourteen miles down the road and collecting it would prove difficult.

Mr Burton thought and then said, 'I'll tell you what I'll do, I'll give you a lift down there myself on the combination. Don't worry about the insurance; I can organise an AA Insurance cover note for you for a few days.'

'Is that allowed?' said Robert.

'Nobody will notice,' said Mr Burton, 'the area office is down at Plymouth and if anybody does notice, they'll reckon I'm giving you a lift back to your car after a breakdown or something.'

'OK then, Mr Burton, I'm ready when you are,' responded Robert with enthusiasm.

Mr Burton crushed out the butt of his cigarette beneath his steel-shod boot, put on his helmet goggles and gauntlets, and swung his leg over the bike. He turned to Robert and indicated for him to mount behind him, and kick-started the bike. Robert had thought that he might have been able to travel in the sidecar. However, that was full of tools for car mechanics and he had to ride pillion. He crouched forward behind Mr Burton, placed his feet on the rear foot rests and gripped the back of the rear seat with his hands.

The combination pulled away down Priory Road in the direction of Liskeard. Robert lowered his head even more when they picked up speed, to avoid the wind streaming in his eyes, and turned his head to view the passing scenery. The combination was a fairly stable ride unlike the previous single bike pillion rides he had endured when you really had to lean into the motion of the bike in order to remain stable on the road, and where the driver was king and you had no option other than to rely on his riding skills! They reached about forty miles an hour and the combination purred on relentlessly. Robert noticed an AA box that they had just passed. These boxes were a bit of a mystery to him, but he understood that if you were a member, you were given a key that allowed you access to them and inside you would find a telephone with which you could phone the AA for assistance with your motoring difficulties.

They reached the outskirts of Liskeard and Mr Burton drove the combination into the depot. They dismounted and walked into the office. A blonde girl was there typing and manning the telephone, otherwise it was very quiet. 'You're back already then, Mr Burton,' she said.

'Yes, Lu,' he said, 'an emergency here with young Robert. Make us some coffee please, love, before I sort out a bike for him.'

The two men lit up cigarettes and drained the coffee cups.

'Thanks love, that was just what the doctor ordered. Come on then, Robert, let's find that bike.'

They found it at the back end of the depot garage and wheeled it out into the sunshine at the front. Remarkably the tyres were still up to correct pressure after all those months of disuse. The bike was pulled back on to its stand and Mr Burton checked it over for any anomalies. Apart from being very dusty, it appeared to be in good condition – but would it start?

Mr Burton straddled the bike and kick-started it again and again, but it would not start. He topped up the petrol tank and tried again. It coughed and spluttered but still would not start. He adjusted the timing lever and set it to top dead centre (tdc). It still would not start up properly, and he continued to adjust the timing. He set it to a couple of degrees before tdc and kick-started it and it finally burst into life. He grinned at Robert as he adjusted the throttle and got the bike ticking over nicely.

Robert breathed a sigh of relief. Thank goodness it works! he thought. The bike was switched off and they walked back into the office.

'Sort out some insurance for that bike for Robert, please, love,' said Mr Burton, addressing the girl.

She got out the paperwork and filled in the cover note with all the details. 'That will be five pounds then please for a fortnight,' she said to Robert.

Robert paid up and returned with Mr Burton to the bike. 'There you are then, boy, safe journey back to Bodmin and a good trip out tonight.'

'Thank you very much for your help, Mr Burton. I will take good care of the bike.' Robert straddled the bike, kick-started it and it started up straight away.

'Try it round the local estate before you go back,' said Mr Burton, just to familiarise yourself with it.'

Robert let the clutch in and pulled away slowly, waved to Mr Burton and drove into the local estate road, changing up to second. He pottered around the local estate roads, re-familiarising himself with driving a motorcycle and gradually feeling more confident, pulled out on the main road back to Bodmin. He opened up the throttle, kicked the gears up to top and roared along the road. It was exhilarating, the open road, the wind through his hair, the speed. Unfortunately, he had no goggles and he had to screw up his eyes to reduce the wind's abrasion to them, making the water from his eyes run down his cheeks. Even in this sunny weather, his hands were cooling down without the benefit of gloves. Ah well, he thought, I don't have too far to drive, even tonight, and I guess I can get by without the goggles and gloves!

Arriving back at Bodmin in Castle Hill next to his aunt's house, he had not found it easy to park the bike, due to the steep hill, and had difficulty in getting it stable on the stand. I know, he thought, I'll get into Aunt's back yard and park it there. Hilda's back yard was slate flagstoned and not particularly large. It did not attract too much sunlight but Hilda's washing line was there nevertheless, and drying of clothes did seem to happen there. It was the ideal spot to park the bike, but Robert would have to get it in there. He walked into the house. Hilda was not in at that time and he went straight through to the back yard and opened the back gate that was normally bolted from the inside. He went back to the bike and kick-started it. It would have been impossible for him to wheel it back up the hill to the yard entrance, so he drove it round the block, stopped outside the back yard door and reversed the bike into the yard. He killed the engine, pulled it up on to the stand, closed the yard door, bolted it and entered the house via the back door. He went to the lounge to await the arrival of his aunt and noticed that the church clock hands were nearly at twelve thirty as far as he could make out, and the time was confirmed by the clock bell striking the half hour. He sat down in his favourite armchair and lit up a cigarette.

Aunt Hilda returned and Robert had to explain the motorbike to her. She was not too bothered, being a motoring woman herself, but if his mother knew, she would have been beside herself with worry over Robert's safety. His aunt was quite happy with the bike parked in the back yard, as long as it did not drip oil, and Robert was very attentive in placing a drip tray under the sump just in case. He could not have his aunt slipping up on a slippery surface and further damaging herself!

Hilda prepared lunch and again, Robert was very well fed. Afterwards they retired to the lounge with their cups of tea where Robert told Hilda of his chance meeting with Mr Burton and the ensuing outcome of the ride to Liskeard and the return journey with the bike.

'Well, you be careful when you drive out there tonight my dear, it will be dark coming back and you have no goggles or helmet or anything apart from your daytime clothes.'

'Yes,' said Robert, 'I will exercise maximum care!'

The afternoon wore on and Hilda and Robert relaxed in the lounge with their tea but Robert's thoughts were continually on this evening's meeting with Juliet in spite of the general conversational topics he discussed with his aunt that afternoon.

Chapter Nine

Saturday evening had arrived. Robert had smartened himself up for the outing. He had put a collar and tie on, and his green corduroy jacket, cavalry twill trousers and heavy brogue shoes. They should be warm enough for riding in at night and if he did fall off for any reason, the fairly thick cloth of the jacket and trousers should serve as some sort of protection.

Heaven forbid that he should fall off though, as he was aware what damage even grazing could do to the body as one slid down a road. He had heard reported experiences from some of his friends who had had the misfortune of motorcycle spills, incurring some damage to their bodies. Mercifully their injuries were not life-threatening and had healed up well. But it was a salutary experience to learn of such things, and Robert, when driving, had always exercised full caution over his bike control. You could not, however, always account for wet roads and metal drain covers. Robert himself had come off bikes in the past under such wet conditions but was lucky enough to end up on grass verges which had cushioned his falls!

He opened up the back gate. Hilda stood at the door whilst Robert mounted the bike. She said, 'Don't worry about the back gate, I'll leave it unbolted for you and you can get the bike back in here later tonight. You do have your front door key with you, don't you, my dear?'

'Yes Aunt, I do, thanks.' Robert kick-started the bike and it erupted into life. It sounded very loud in the confined yard and Robert saw his aunt wince. He turned to her, said cheerio and pulled out from the yard, across the pavement, and carefully crossed the road, turning right to go up Castle Hill. Hilda closed the back gate and re-entered the house and went to finish off tidying up the tea things, thinking that Robert and Juliet would probably make a very nice couple.

Robert revved up the throttle, kicked the bike up from its low gear to second and proceeded up Castle Hill. He was doing about thirty when he reached the top of the hill and set out onto the moor, passing the camping site at the top end of the town and changing up to top as his speed increased. He was following the route that he and Hilda had taken on Thursday, past Racecourse Farm and Racecourse Down, past Cardingham and towards Temple. The bike handled very well and he found it even more exhilarating going across the moor than the previous run from Liskeard to Bodmin.

The road junction with the sign pointing right to Temple was approaching and he turned off left towards the direction of St Breward. The signpost to Treswigga came up and Robert turned the bike carefully left to Metherin, and then he was approaching the gravelled courtyard to the entrance of Mentreaths Farm. He turned in and slowed down considerably to cross the gravel, knowing how 'skiddy' it was, and came to a halt a shade before the portico entrance. Robert switched the bike off and sat for a moment collecting his thoughts. All was silent. The porch light was on already. A bit early, thought Robert, it's not dark yet and they'll be running out of oil soon if they are not careful. He got off the bike and pulled it up on to its stand, and walked slowly towards the portico entrance, pushing his disrupted hair back into place. Even hair oil could not hold it in place on a motorbike!

The front door was not ajar this time and he pulled down on the bell pull, listening to the clanging of the hall bell and looking at the brass plaque on the door with its inscription, 'Mentreaths Farm', while he waited. However, the farm was generally known as Tall Chimneys from the obvious feature of its tall chimneys which were easily observed from all directions around here.

The door opened and Leon stood there. 'Robert, come in, my boy Anne is waiting for you, do come on in.' Leon had not yet cottoned on to Juliet using her other given name as Juliet! 'Where are you going tonight?' he said.

'Jamaica Inn,' responded Robert.

'That sounds fine,' said Leon. 'Alice and I often went there in our early days, I would like to go there again sometime, and I expect that it has not changed too much.'

They walked into the parlour and Juliet was sitting there

waiting. She stood up when Robert and Leon entered the room, and looked towards Robert and smiled. Robert said 'Hello Juliet, you're looking fine,' and observed her blue dress with the full skirt and the waistband and the cardigan draped over her shoulders. Her earrings sparkled, as did her wrist band, and her hair was curled back around her ears. She does look stunning, thought Robert. I hope she will be warm enough on the bike!

Leon had heard Robert say 'Juliet', but overlooked it as they all walked to the front door. 'Have a good time and drive carefully. Not too late back now,' he cautioned. Leon closed the front door behind them and Robert and Juliet crossed the threshold of the portico and turned towards the bike.

Juliet stopped in her tracks – a motorbike! She had not expected this, rather anticipating a car. Robert sensed her reaction and broke in with, 'I'm sorry about the bike, Juliet, I'm sure that you were expecting a car!' He gave a rapid explanation as to how it all came about.

'That's fine, Robert,' she said, 'I'm quite happy to ride pillion and we have not got too far to go. You know that I'm used to riding a lot, horses of course – though not in these clothes – so I'm a rugged sort of girl.' She smiled at him.

Reassured, Robert grinned back and said, 'That's good then, let's get the old machine on the road.' He mounted the bike, eased it off the stand, kick-started it and gently revved the engine. He turned to Juliet and motioned for her to climb up behind him. She did so, gathering her skirt around her legs and trapping the excess under her seat.

Robert said, 'Put your feet onto the rear foot rests and when we start moving, lean into my back and follow the motion of the bike. When I lean left or right, lean with me, you must follow the motion of the bike for a smooth ride.'

'Yes Robert,' she said, and slipped her arms around his waist and leaned into his back. Robert felt the warmth of her body up close to him and realised that this felt good. He kicked the bike into first gear, turned the it around, circling on the gravel, drove through the gate and turned right up the hill towards Treswigga, then followed the road towards Temple.

Having reached the junction with the main road, they turned

left in the direction signposted towards Bolventor. Robert moved up through the gears to top and the bike purred along, crossing this short section of the moor. The sun was streaming down, enhancing the moorland views and throwing up the distant tors in stark relief. How exhilarating this is, thought Robert, particularly with someone such as Juliet snuggling up behind me.

As though in response to his thoughts, Juliet tightened her grip around his waist. The buildings of Jamaica Inn loomed up ahead of them and Robert began to slow the bike, going down through the gears. On his approach he noticed the sign to Dozmary Pool and decided on a short diversion to it. He brought the bike to a standstill beside the lake and turned to Juliet. 'Dozmary Pool,' he said, 'thought we'd have a quick look before going in to the pub.'

The evening shadows were lengthening and the lake lay before them in all its stark, quiet splendour, with the sunlight playing on the water. The water was flat and so silent as to be unnerving. There was a farm building beside the lake and Robert wondered how people could live in such a quiet, remote spot. Then he thought of the Arthurian legend associated with Dozmary Pool, in which the Lady of the Lake had risen from the waters to receive the sword, Excalibur. He scanned the lake and in response to its desolation shuddered involuntarily. He turned to Juliet and said, 'That's enough of Dozmary then, let's get to the pub.'

He turned the bike around and drove off back to Jamaica Inn. He turned left off the road into the courtyard of the inn through the broad entrance in the sturdy, stone perimeter wall. The bike shuddered to a halt. Robert turned to Juliet and said, 'Are you all right to dismount now?'

She said she was and swung herself off the back of the bike, straightened herself up, pulled her cardigan closer around her shoulders and waited for Robert. He pulled the bike back onto its stand, brushed his hair back with a sweep of his hand and turned to Juliet. 'Into the inn then,' said Robert, playing on words.

Juliet caught his humour, smiled at him and he led her into the inn through the main stone porch and into the lounge bar. It was quiet with only two other people in the bar, sitting back from the fireplace. A log fire was burning, but it was not a great roar, rather it was at a low ebb. Juliet moved to sit at the table in front of the fireplace; she was a little cold from the bike ride and welcomed the warmth of the fire. The later August evenings were chilling down a little as the year moved towards September. Robert joined her and sat down at the table. There was no sign of the landlord for the moment.

Robert said, 'It's very quiet, hardly a person in here apart from that couple over there.'

'It's Saturday,' said Juliet, 'and it's a changeover day for visitors – they are either travelling to or from home or settling into their holiday accommodation.'

'Of course,' said Robert, 'that's it, I guess. What would you like to drink?'

'Just an orange juice, please,' she responded.

'Can't I persuade you with anything stronger?'

'No thank you, Robert, I'm not at all a drinker and it goes to my head so easily. I get quite giddy if I have anything stronger.'

Robert looked towards the bar. No sign of anybody yet. He gazed around the room. There were lots of interesting curios on the mantelpiece and a fine old grandfather clock was nestling against the wall away from the fire. The ceiling was oak-beamed with horse brasses attached and lots of pewter pots were hanging from the beam that crossed the ceiling above the fireplace.

'It's an interesting place with lots of atmosphere,' said Robert.

'Yes,' said Juliet, 'I have not been out here since I was a child and from my memory it does not seemed to have changed too much.'

'Good evening sir, madam, can I help you?'

Robert jumped to his feet – the landlord had arrived at last.

'What would you like, sir?'

'An orange juice and a pint of your best bitter please,' said Robert. 'Oh, and a couple of packets of crisps as well.'

'Thank you sir, that will be one shilling and ten pence.'

Robert gave him a florin, received the change of tuppence and carried the drinks across to the table. He returned to retrieve the crisps. The landlord slipped away behind the bar, not to be seen again easily.

'I wonder,' said Robert, 'if he's up to some smuggling racket. Seems a quiet cove to me.'

Juliet chuckled at this inference. 'Oh, I'm sure he's not,' she said. 'I don't think that goes on here now.'

Robert, ever the speculator on such matters, went on to embroider a tale including the landlord having connections with the pirates of Penzance and operating a smuggling ring that included the bigwigs of Bodmin. He had Juliet in fits of laughter over this and Robert was pleased that she could share his sense of humour. Robert drank from his pint. 'That's refreshing,' he said, 'that's a good pint. Have not had such a good one for a while.'

Juliet sipped her orange juice. He opened a crisp packet and searched for the little twist bag of salt. Finding it, he opened the twist bag, scattered the contents into the bag, clasped the neck of the bag shut and shook it vigorously to distribute the salt evenly over the crisps. He offered the bag to Juliet and she took out two or three crisps and ate them one by one. Crisps always went down well with a pint, the saltiness increasing the thirst and creating a consequent desire for more drink.

Robert and Juliet were getting along well and opening up on new tracks of conversation and new subjects. They had eyes only for one another. That was not difficult under the circumstances of such a quiet pub, but it was more than that – an indefinable bond was growing between them. Towards the end of the evening, Robert even blurted out that he would very much like Juliet to meet his parents one day, next time she was in London.

'Yes, Robert,' she looked at him very warmly, 'I would like that very much. As you know, I go up occasionally to visit relatives there and could extend my stay sometime so as to meet your parents.'

That's fine, then,' said Robert. 'I'll organise it when I get back there. When I return from staying with my aunt. I hope soon to be getting into employment with an engineering firm, and when I'm settled I'll invite you up.'

Juliet smiled in response and nodded her head in agreement. She had met his parents a long time previously when they had stayed at Hilda's, but she was of course quite young and had only distant memories of them.

'Time, ladies and gentlemen, please,' came the cry from the distant 'pirate' landlord.

Robert said, 'He's getting rid of us now so that he can carry on with his clandestine smuggling activities. It must be more lucrative than running this pub.'

Juliet laughed.

'Come on, we had better go now,' he said.

They walked out of the bar and it was quite cool by now, and quite dark. Juliet put her cardigan on fully and clasped her arms across her chest as if feeling the cold. Robert buttoned his jacket up to the top. It was dark but the sky was clear, and the myriad star formations were breathtaking to look at. I wonder, thought Robert, why we do not regard these wonders more often. I suppose we are shut up in our little houses in our little towns and we just don't go out to look at these marvels. The immenseness of the open night sky made him feel extremely small, and if light travelled at 186,000 miles a second then those distant stars are an amazing distance away he pondered. They both stopped and looked up together and paused, 'catching the moment' so to speak.

Robert then walked to the bike, thinking that there must be a reason for everything, pulled the bike off the stand and kick-started it. It burst into action after two or three kicks, as it had been cold. He turned to Juliet and found she was already climbing on. 'I see that you're getting used to this bike then, quite the professional now.'

She slid up against him and clasped her arms warmly around his waist. Robert eventually found the light switch and was relieved when they switched on. He dipped the beam and they pulled out of the yard of the inn and set off on their return journey.

It was very dark crossing the moor. A mist had descended, throwing back the headlight beam, and Robert had to proceed with caution, as it was difficult to see far ahead. It was particularly difficult to see the road signs and they pulled to a halt more than once to check the signs at close scrutiny. It was comforting to have Juliet with him under these circumstances! They came to the St Breward sign and he turned the bike off the road to the right and slowly retraced the route to Tall Chimneys Farm. Robert was going dead slow now as the mist was pretty thick at the bottom of the hill, but he did catch the entrance to Tall Chimneys reflected in the headlight and turned slowly across the crunchy gravel. The portico lamp was still on, giving extra illumination. Robert brought the bike to a halt.

Juliet leapt off the back. 'Thank you for a most wonderful evening, Robert.'

Robert turned towards her.

'We'll arrange to meet up again before you go back,' she said and their lips met for a brief moment, and then she was off to the front door and vanished in! He thought that, that was a rapid departure but comforted himself with the thought that it was definite that they would meet again. He would have relished her lips lingering longer against his, but that was that, and he turned the bike to leave the drive of the farm. It was difficult and slow getting back up the minor roads from the farm under the misty conditions, and he was pleased to arrive at the main road turning back to town. He turned right and progressed on towards Bodmin, slowly carefully. Not really a night to be out driving across the moors, he thought, but things were different now. Juliet was there!

He was comforted to see the few twinkling lights still on in the old town of Bodmin and progressed steadily down Castle Hill until he reached his aunt's house and stopped the bike outside the rear gate. True to her promise, Hilda had left the gate open and he backed the bike in with difficulty and set it on its stand. He closed the gate behind him and walked round to the front of the house. He let himself in the front door with the key his aunt had given him, walked through the hall to the back door, went out and bolted the back gate. He walked back past the bike, patting it on the seat, entered through and locked the back door, crept up the stairs in the dark, found the door to his room, threw his clothes off onto the chair and crashed into bed.

Chapter Ten

Ding-dong, ding-dong, ding-dong, ding... The ringing of St Petroc's bells penetrated into Robert's consciousness. He roused himself. Ding-dong, ding-dong... Why were they ringing so insistently? he thought. It's not a national emergency, is it? It then came to him – it was Sunday morning and of course the bells were ringing to call the faithful to church. He lay there intoxicated by their melodious ringing, reaching deep into his inner consciousness as though nothing mattered any more, only that their cry be heard.

Knock-knock, knock-knock, knock-knock. Only the insistent knocking at the door distracted Robert from the ringing bells. He realised that it must be his aunt at the door. 'Come in, come in,' he shouted out, and Hilda walked in with the tea tray.

'Hello my dear, I thought that you were still asleep, as I was getting no answer.'

'Well, it's the bells, Aunt; I was listening to the bells.'

'Magnificent, aren't they?' she said. 'Those bell-ringers do a sterling job, they practise a lot and are top ringers in this area. How did you get on last night with An— Juliet, I mean?' as she corrected herself.

'Oh, fine, Aunt,' he responded, 'very enjoyable.' He went on to give her a resume of the evening. 'We hope to meet again in my last week here, but the exact time and date has yet to be arranged.'

'Lovely girl she is,' commented Hilda, 'a bit like my own daughter, would make somebody a fine wife someday.'

Robert realised that they had met up more often, then, than he had hitherto imagined. 'She certainly would,' said Robert, thinking that here was a possibility!

Hilda diverted her attention to the bells and to church. 'I'm going to the ten o'clock service this morning,' she said. 'Do you want to come with me?'

Robert thought for a moment and then responded in the affirmative. He knew that she would never force anyone to go. 'Is there communion this week?' he said.

'Not this week,' replied Hilda, 'but it's the hymn and prayer sandwich.' She used this colloquialism to describe the Church of England service that alternated between hymn, then prayer or reading, and then hymn again. Hilda looked very pleased that Robert had decided to come, and Robert guessed she would certainly show him off to certain parties within the church!

Hilda walked out of the room, content. 'I'll be preparing breakfast soon, Robert, come down when you are ready.'

Robert got up and dressed appropriately for church, with collar and tie and sports jacket. He had no suit with him, so the sports jacket and trousers would have to do.

Because of the shortage of time before the start of the service, Hilda had actually prepared a lighter breakfast of scrambled eggs on toast and they would thus be through with it much quicker. Robert enjoyed this for a change and began eating it whilst Hilda went off to dress in her Sunday best. By the time she had returned, he had finished his breakfast and was ready to accompany her to church. She certainly could dress smartly when she wanted, thought Robert, as he observed her in her light-blue suit and wide-brimmed hat. Goodness, he thought, she certainly had similar characteristics to his mother when dressing up was in order. Often he thought that they modelled themselves on the royal family, particularly the Queen Mother when it came to dressing up! He complimented her on how smart she looked, and that pleased her no end.

They walked slowly off down the garden path on their way to St Petroc's, Hilda holding on to Robert's arm to steady herself against any slippery surface underfoot. They progressed slowly down to the church steps and carefully up them, past St Guron's well on the way to the main church door. Entering the porch, they were presented with hymn books and books of common prayer by the church wardens either side of the entrance, who nodded in recognition of Hilda. 'Not on the organ today then Mrs Yudy' said one of them.

'No, not today, Lennard,' she replied. 'It's not my Sunday for that this time, and besides, I have my nephew with me this morning.'

They shook Robert's hand and welcomed him to St Petroc's and hoped that he would enjoy his stay in Bodmin. Robert and Hilda proceeded to her favourite seating area on the left-hand side of the church in front of the lectern. Here she could hear and see the preacher remarkably well. They both sat down and Hilda glanced around at the rest of the congregation, nodding and smiling to the faces she recognised. Robert sat fairly impassively with his own thoughts and waited for the service to start.

The organ started up. The vicar processed in, preceded by the cross bearer and followed by his curate and eight choirboys in their red tunics and white surplices with the choirmaster in similar costume. The congregation stood up and the organ started up the introduction to the first hymn. 'For all the saints who from their labours rest...' It was fairly belted out by the congregation. A good rousing hymn that was guaranteed to wake anybody up from their slumbers. The following reading was from St John's Gospel, chapter six. Like the hearers of Jesus' words, Robert could not fully understand how one could obtain eternal life by eating his body and drinking his blood – was this not sheer cannibalism?

The next hymn was, 'O God our help in ages past our hope for years to come...', one of the great John Wesley classics, followed by prayers from the revised Book of Common Prayer. Thumbing through the prayer book earlier before the start of the service, Robert had cast his eye over the '39 Articles', and was quite struck with their vehement abhorrence of the Catholic mass and yet he had found the family of his Catholic college chum, Charles, most charming. I'm sure it could not be that bad, he thought, if it produced such good people! Prayers were read for the good governance of the kingdom and for the monarch. They all settled back then for the vicar's sermon. Mr Reginald Knight, MA Oxon, was an impressive figure. He stood a full six feet tall and had a shock of wiry grey hair. His war medal ribbons were displayed on the left-hand side of his surplice, indicating his war service. Certain men after the war had taken up the ministry as a result of their particular experiences.

His voice boomed to the back of the church and made everybody sit up and listen. His theme was 'love your enemies as yourself and do good to those who persecute you'. Not an easy thing to live up to, thought Robert. The service continued and the final rousing hymn, 'To be a pilgrim' was sung. Very inspiring that hymn was, thought Robert. The vicar and his entourage processed out to the vestry with the final hymn still playing. The singing ceased with the end of the hymn and it was the acceptable time for the organist to explore her repertoire, bursting into paeans of additional organ music in an endeavour to outdo her rivals!

'That Miss Probey, showing off again,' whispered Hilda to Robert. 'Just because she studied music at Cambridge, she thinks she's better than anybody else.' Hilda was obviously one of the rivals!

They stood up from their seats and Hilda made a beeline for the curate who had disrobed from his surplice by now. She spoke animatedly to him and then gestured to Robert to join them. The curate was thin, pale faced and had thin, sandy hair and was of average height. Hilda had to look up to him whilst Robert towered over him. The two men were introduced and spoke together with conversational pleasantries. Robert always thought that people in such positions were older than him but the curate was probably much closer to Robert's age than he could have imagined. His aunt was most respectful and taken up with him as she was with all clergy. However, Robert reserved his judgement on him, considering him rather effete and not fully to his liking. Goodness, thought Robert, I have just exited from a church service and I am judging people already!

Hilda and Robert moved slowly towards the church porch, exchanging pleasantries with folk as they passed. The vicar was shaking hands with people just as they left through the main church door. Hilda said to him, 'You and your curate must come up again for lunch sometime, but I cannot invite you today as my nephew and I are going down Porth way today.'

'Thank you, Mrs Yudy, you are most generous with your hospitality and we'll be pleased to come when convenient.' He tuned to Robert. 'And this is your nephew, then. Welcome to St Petroc's.'

Robert replied, 'Thank you vicar, pleased to meet you. Excellent sermon today, lots of food for thought there – I must certainly improve.'

The vicar chuckled. 'We can all do that,' he responded.

Robert warmed to him. He was a man's sort of man, which was no doubt partly due to his wartime service. Robert proffered him a Players cigarette. 'No thank you, I'm a pipe man myself.'

Robert lit up his cigarette and inhaled deeply, exhaling the smoke away from Hilda and the vicar into the bright morning air.

'Well vicar, we must be on our way. It's the first of the month communion service next Sunday, so I should be present at the eight o'clock service then,' said Hilda.

'Bye for now,' said the vicar.

Robert and Hilda walked away as the vicar turned to others waiting to talk with him.

They made their way slowly back up Castle Hill. Robert said, 'Doesn't Miss Sandow or her mother ever go to St Petroc's?'

'No, no, my dear,' replied Hilda as if this would have been beyond the bounds of possibility, 'as you know, she plays at St Neot's out on the moor and her mother sometimes goes with her. There's no likelihood of her changing now! I don't know what the attraction is other than that she's sole organist out there and likes to be wanted.' She chuckled. They turned into the garden gate, Robert dropped his cigarette end into the nearby drain opening and they proceeded up the garden path into the house.

It was a pasty and tomato chutney lunch again, followed by mixed fruit and scalded cream before they prepared for the trip down to Porth. Robert went upstairs and selected some suitable clothes, not forgetting his swimming trunks and beach towel, retrieved his shaving gear from the bathroom, threw it all into his grip bag and returned downstairs to join Hilda.

'Got everything, my dear?'

'Yes, thank you, Aunt.'

They walked slowly across to Miss Mudge's to get the car. The farmyard was deserted apart from a couple of chickens wandering aimlessly about. The church clock struck one o'clock with one resounding clang. They drove out of the yard and turned right, the indicator indicating the way. They reached the bottom of the hill at St Petroc's and Hilda drove across the junction, up St Nicholas Street and right into Fore Street. They continued up Fore Street and into Bore Street. The town was quiet in the afternoon sun, reflecting a Sunday afternoon typical of any English town. They drove on across the junction into Westheath Avenue, passing the Catholic church on the left-hand side and the asylum on the right. They were now on the way to Newquay but more particularly Porth. It was about a twenty-mile journey and Robert relaxed back into his seat and reflected on all that had happened since his arrival down here. He particularly reflected on his meetings with Juliet.

The car went through Lanivet at about twenty-five miles per hour and continued onwards, approaching Goss Moor, passed the left-hand turn to Roche, where the hermit's dwelling was situated on top of Roche Rock, continued under the railway bridge and onto Goss Moor. Hilda had put the car up to her top speed of forty mph and roared across the moor. Robert sat back awaiting the arrival of Indian Queens. The name of this little town always fascinated him, but he had no idea of the origins of the name. They turned right at the Indian Queens junction and joined St Columb Road. They went through Mount Joy and on to Quintrel Downs where they turned right towards St Columb Minor. Hilda missed the right-hand turning to this village, but took the next turning to Porth.

Turning in there, Roberts got the inevitable butterflies again. His young days spent at Porth with his cousins and aunts had such good memories for him that he thrilled even on the approach there. They slowly motored down the hill to the bay, through the narrow lanes with overhanging trees, and Robert caught glimpses of Porth Island as they descended. Hilda sensed his anticipation and said 'It's grand to be back, isn't it?'

Robert remained silent and did not reply. The car drew under the Porth road bridge, past Old Bridge House on the right, past the entrance to 'Morvah,' his uncle's residence, past the entrance steps to Porth's post office and turned right past Aunt Aggie's front door and immediately left, halting to face the sea wall overlooking the bay next to Aunt Aggie's garden seat.

They walked over to the green painted door with the sign 'Post Office' fixed to it. Aunt Aggie was sub-postmistress, but this was the entrance to her adjoining apartment. The door was open and they walked into the vestibule and up its sand-dusted concrete steps. The fine sand from the beach surface was ever blown around here under doors and carried around underfoot. The vestibule reminded Robert so much of his beaching days as a youngster, and he knew the exact corner where the buckets and spades were kept after a morning or afternoon on the beach. They entered through the inner door turning left to Aggie's apartment door. On the right was her entrance to the post office, partitioned off with a heavy red curtain that also hid the tanks for the paraffin oil. They knocked on the door and entered, and Aggie was up out of her chair in an instant.

'My dears both,' she exclaimed, 'I heard the car draw up and I knew it was you.' She embraced both of them saying, 'Lovely to see you again, come and sit yourselves down and I'll get the kettle on.'

Hilda sat in the other available armchair and Robert sat himself at the dining table under the window and caught the magnificent view out across the sea wall, across the beach to Porth Island and to the incoming tide. This sight always thrilled him more than anybody ever knew. It must be probably the most amazing view encountered anywhere in the world; at least, it always was to him.

Aggie had gone over to put the kettle on to the top of the coal fired range and then reseated herself in her armchair next to Hilda. This was Aggie's apartment, with one living room, and a kitchen-diner. The door opposite Robert opened into a long corridor that led to an intersecting door that opened to Uncle Jack's home, Morvah, where he lived with Aunt Gi and their sons, Robert's cousins. Off this corridor to the left were Aggie's two bedrooms.

The conversation sparkled between them all, ebbing and flowing over family matters and catching up on developments and events. When Aggie and Hilda spoke more together, he contented himself with the view out of the window. The kettle boiled and Aggie moved to make the tea. The tea was most refreshing, accompanied with Cornish splits lashed with cream and syrup. The expression for this combination was 'Thunder and Lightning', and its effects on one's taste buds were considered not dissimilar to such an elemental combination!

'That was delicious. Thank you very much, Aunt Aggs,' said Robert.

'Yes,' said Hilda, 'that was really something special, Agatha, haven't had Thunder and Lightning for ages!' The tea things were cleared away and their conversation carried on.

Then came a knock on the corridor door and Jack entered, Robert's uncle. He was still flushed from bending over a hot stove and was wearing his long, white, starched apron. He did the evening dinners for the visitors, those people whom they had to rely on for summer income. He had his pipe clamped between his teeth. Robert noticed the distinct slot that had been worn between the upper and lower incisors after all the years of accommodating his pipe.

'Hello, my dears,' he said. 'My word, boy, you are looking well and grown-up. Proper man you are now. Hilda, good to see you again maid, how is my favourite town, Bodmin?'

The appropriate responses were made and general conversation ensued, with Jack sucking and blowing on his pipe. 'Well my dears, I must get back to the stove, plenty to do to keep the visitors happy. Pop up and see us during your stay, Rob, and I dare say you will be seeing Simeon and John 'fore too long.' With this he made his farewells unceremoniously and turned and left.

'My,' said Hilda, 'that boy does work hard,' referring to Jack, 'just to keep those boys at Cathedral School.'

'I know,' said Aggie, 'but you can't tell him to slow down, can you? I tried often enough myself.'

Robert remained impassive, not being drawn in the conversation. His thoughts were on when he would be meeting up with his cousins and what they would be getting up to.

'Well,' said Hilda, 'I'd better go up and see Gi before I go. Not much chance of her popping down here!' She went up the corridor to meet up with Robert's Aunt Gi in that Morvah's kitchen.

Aggie turned to Robert and said how she had looked forward to him coming to stay and would be pleased to look after him. Aggie was Hilda's younger sister, was unmarried and not likely to marry. She was a most dedicated servant of the post office and was a most respected long-term resident of Porth. She was consulted for her advice and sympathy by many a local and visitor alike. The most tragic of things was when she had to offer sympathy to people who had lost relatives in drowning accidents. These were rare but did happen due to the vicious undertow caused by the river that ran out on to the beach under the incoming rising tide. Robert remembered once that he and his cousins, as young boys, were in the sea in the wrong place and Aggie had rushed out fully clothed into the sea to bring them out. The lifeguard was there to advise, but Aggie was not taking any chances!

Hilda returned. 'Well, Gi is in the thick of it as well as Jack, serving up the dinners to the visitors. Simeon and John are out at a football match in Truro and will return late,' she said, turning to Robert, 'and I dare say that you probably won't be seeing them until tomorrow evening after work.'

Robert thought, Work, yes, they are at work unlike me who has just completed university. Ah well, I'll soon be in the thick of it myself, he mused when I return to London.

Hilda said, 'I must be getting back to Bodmin before it gets too dark – I will be down next Saturday to pick you up Robert. Bye bye, my dears.'

Robert breathed an inward sigh of relief – at least I won't have to go back on the train! he thought. Robert and Aggie accompanied her out to the car and after much huffing and puffing with car reversing Hilda got to the corner of the post office and with a final wave was off up the hill towards St Columb.

Aggie and Robert moved over to the sea wall and observed the tide coming in to the bay. To the left was the Lusty Glaze headland on which 'Glendorgal' the Victorian gentleman's seaside residence, now a hotel, was built and to the right, the larger headland of Trevelgue Head, 'The Island', with its hill-top fort jutted out into the Atlantic. The views were truly stunning, more so since the sun was starting to make its downward journey, seemingly about to plunge into the sea! Aggie said, 'It's getting chilly now, let's go inside, Robbie.'

They walked in and sat at the table under the window and watched the sun complete its journey into the sea. They talked on, having supper drinks until it was time for bed. Aggie said,

'Well it's Monday tomorrow and I have to open up the post office at 9 a.m., so I had better not be too late to bed.'

Taking the hint, Robert said, 'No, of course not, Aunt,' and went and retrieved his grip bag from the vestibule and said, 'Usual room, Aunt?'

'Yes my dear, you know where it is and it's all made up.' Robert did indeed know where it was and to get to it you had to go through Aggie's room. It had no facilities of its own apart from an old washstand and basin, so it was better to use the facilities just off the vestibule before retiring and to clean your teeth at Aunt Aggie's kitchen sink. 'I'm off to bed then, Aunt, good night.'

'Goodnight then, my dear, you'll see Simeon and John tomorrow, sleep well.'

Robert walked through Aggie's bedroom into his. The bed was under the window, the foot of the bed facing the door. Robert unpacked his grip and placed his things in the chest of drawers and his shaving gear on to the marble top of the washstand. He dressed in his pyjamas and slipped into the bed. The sash window was open and the curtains stirred imperceptibly in the breeze. The moonlight penetrated into the room and onto the opposite wall. He lay back in the bed and listened to the gentle purring of the surf on the sand up against the sea wall. Having reached that far in the bay, it had dissipated most of its Atlantic power by then, thought Robert. I wonder how Juliet is getting on? he thought. It seemed like an age since he had last seen her.

Chapter Eleven

Robert awoke. There was no immediate sound of surf but only a distant roar from a faraway sea. The tide had retreated in the night and was no longer at the sea wall, and the effect of its distant roar was as if one held a large seashell to one's ear and listened. The sun streamed in through the window.

Another fine day, thought Robert, and he turned to look at his watch on the bedside table. Nine fifteen. That was good, he thought. Aunt Aggie would be in the post office by now and he could therefore walk through her bedroom, use the facilities, wash and shave at the kitchen sink without being disturbed. He knew that later he could use the bathroom at Uncle Jack's, but that was best left to the evenings, when the visitors were out of the way.

Robert completed his ablutions and dressed in casual clothes suitable for the beach. He had decided that he would spend that day wandering around the bay re-familiarising himself with all his favourite spots. He walked through to Aggie's kitchen-diner and saw that a place had been laid for him at the table for breakfast. He could help himself to cereals, boil eggs, and make toast and tea. It would make a nice change from the big Bodmin fry-ups! He thought though that he ought to check with Aggie before he started, to ensure that this was her intention – for him to help himself. He pulled back the red curtain covering the entrance to the post office and saw Aggie behind the counter, speaking to a customer. He looked around at the interior of the post office. As well as a post office, it was a beach shop and store for particular commodities that otherwise one would have to purchase in Newquay, a distance away. It was like Aladdin's cave and Robert remembered when young that Aggie would give him free rein in the shop to help himself to any item that he might be attracted to. Such things as penknives with that spike attachment for getting stones out of horses' hooves were of a particular interest to him.

Each year that he had previously stayed there was a free choice, but by now he had undoubtedly grown out of it.

The customer left and Aggie turned to Robert. 'Morning Robbie, did you sleep well?'

'Yes thanks, Aunt Aggs, very well. Shall I help myself to breakfast?'

'Yes my dear, and when you have finished, come in here and choose something that you might like.'

'OK, thanks, Aunt.' Robert returned to the kitchen-diner and started with cereals, then boiled some eggs and grilled some toast with difficulty in the oven of the old range cooker. It was all washed down with a pot of tea and he sat back sipping tea and admiring the view of the bay through the window.

The door opened and Robert started. 'Good morning, Miss Benney,' came a call and in walked in a very small lady.

'Oh, is Miss Benney in the shop?' she said, and 'You must be Robert.'

'Yes,' he replied, remembering that this little lady in her pinafore was Mrs Curragh, the lady who cleaned for Aggie. 'You have grown since I last saw you,' she said. They had a short conversation and then she said, 'I must be getting on then,' and furiously attacked the brass door handles with a yellow duster.

That's why they are so shiny then! thought Robert. She finished her duties at Aggie's and then moved on to do for Mr and Mrs Benney at Morvah.

With breakfast over, Robert washed up the breakfast things and looked into the post office. 'I'm going to have a wander round the beach, Aunt, and re-familiarise myself with the old place.'

'That's all right, my dear, I'll be cooking for us about tea time, so take something with you before you go.'

'Thanks, Aunt, but I'll probably call in at the beach café for a midday snack if I feel in need of one.' With that, Robert walked out of the post office, through the vestibule and down towards the beach, lighting up a cigarette as he went along. He walked through the breach in the old sea wall and entered the beach, although it was perhaps debatable where the real beach started, as there was so much sand strewn up the road anyway.

He walked on, striding over the rivulets of water that poured on to the beach from the stream that trickled down the road. This was a favourite spot for youngsters to play here. The beach was practically deserted. It was early morning yet and the visitors were never early morning starters! Robert walked on, veering to the left and passing the lifeguard hut on the rocky promontory at the base of the cliff face. He remembered the lifeguard, Arthur, a grizzled Cornishman, and wondered whether he was still a lifeguard. He used to take Robert and his cousins out fishing from the rocks off Porth Island and regaled them with tales of local lore, some quite unsuitable for the ears of young boys! He was characterised in dress by his red singlet and old corduroy trousers, only revealing his swimming costume if absolutely necessary. The costume was old-fashioned even for these days, consisting of a belted one-piece, trunks and singlet combined. He did place the warning flags – red and yellow – on the beach at the designated swimming areas, but Robert could not recollect him dealing with any specific lifesaving activities!

Robert walked on. The yellow sand became white and dry and fine closer to the sea wall but as he progressed, out the sand was still wet from the tide and the rivulets of it pressed hard into the soles of his soft beach shoes. It was an ideal spot for beach cricket and he had played many a game on such a surface in the past with Simeon and John and their friends. The massive gulls were standing in this area and any approach to them was always rebuffed by their moving away. Fearsome creatures, thought Robert, particularly if they could have had a mind to gang up on you, thinking that you might be a provider of food for them!

Robert walked on towards the private cove of Glendorgal. The steps from the hotel came down here to the beach. Robert and his cousins had often played here in the deep sand, luxuriating in the fact that you could sink in it up to your ankles, a most entertaining experience. They were never censured for such activity! One of his goals was to revisit the deep rock pools situated here, in which they used to fish as children. He carefully made his way up the lower sloping cliff area to a rocky plateau and discovered the rock pools. To his surprise, they were much smaller than he remembered. He had visions of their endless depth and used to think that someday he would swim down into them, somewhat like the illustration from *The Water Babies* and would discover secret lairs. He and his cousins had caught many guppies, those little fish that were so attracted to the bait of mussels lying in rock pool fishing nets. Having satisfied himself that these pools still existed, he carefully retraced his steps down the cliff face to the beach and, still on this side of the bay, walked out to the still-retreating tide. As it was a deep bay, the water was shallow and clear and warm for a long way until one reached the much darker, colder, green-blue sea, topped with the relentlessly crashing white-topped waves. Robert had no intention today to go out and meet those stomach-smashing waves but had decided to meet them perhaps tomorrow or another day, and even surf on them.

He walked directly across the beach towards the narrow crevice separating Trevelgue Head on Porth Island from the rest of the headland. In order to get there, he had to remove his shoes and socks, roll up his trouser legs and wade across the river that ran out on to the beach over this side. The river depth varied according to the tide, and could be thigh deep, but here it was just over ankle deep and easily waded. He walked up the beach area and made his way to the crevice entrance, still carrying his shoes and socks. It was difficult to enter as one had to negotiate some deep rock pools, so he continued to do so barefoot. Further into the crevice was the 'wishing well', into which from the bridge above visitors would drop coins, that were assiduously collected by the local boys in the know! Walking barefoot through the pools, avoiding the sharp stones, he came to the entrance to the cavern with the blowing hole. When the tide was out, the locals, including his mother and relatives, used to hold concerts in this cavern, transporting a harmonium across for the music. It must have been quite an effort! he thought.

The blowing hole was a hole in the roof of the cavern which was quite spectacular when the sea was crashing in there, causing great plumes of spray to issue forth from the hole that could be observed by those on the headland. Robert entered the cavern and, sure enough, the blowing hole could be seen. This gave sufficient light into the cavern to show up the insides well. It was spacious and did certainly lend itself to being a concert hall. He shivered, and thought how damp and cool it was in here, and was happier when he had exited into the bright sunlight outside.

He progressed on through the crevice until he reached the standing rocks on Whipsiderry beach. This immediate area was magnificent with its primeval atmosphere, the roar of the surf, the starkness of the rocks against the clear blue sky, the alternate light and dark in the shadow of the rocks and the sand strewn with seaweed and shells. For a moment, he paused and pondered – creation by design or by evolution? He shuddered, then lit up a cigarette and found a dry rock to sit on. He sat there in the sun, puffing away, and thought on Juliet. I suppose that it does not really matter as long as you are happy, he thought, and raised his hopes with the thought of meeting Juliet again in a few days' time.

He looked at his watch and noted that it was getting on for midday by now. He turned to retrace his steps back through the crevice, under the bridge and, with a certain amount of struggling, through the pools again; to come out on the Porth beach side. He sat in the sun again for a while, allowing his feet to dry, then dusted the sand off them and replaced his socks and shoes and rolled down his trouser legs. He walked back down the beach on the river side towards the beach shop, 'Popes', on the Whipsiderry side of the river. Popes was a magnificent emporium that had everything for your beaching needs from buckets and spades and beach balls to surfboards and swimming hats. Robert had a quick look around the store and yes, it was still as impressive as when he was a youngster, although this time he had no need or desire to buy anything.

He walked on across the road bridge over the river. Pausing, he looked down and picked out one or two small trout swimming against the stream and thus remaining stationary. He wondered if they would rise to a fly even at this late end of the summer. He moved away, crossed over the road and entered the Palm Tree Café and ice cream parlour, and took a seat overlooking the beach back along the old sea wall towards where he had entered. There were a few people in for afternoon tea or a late lunch, but the place was by no means full. He ordered coffee and two Danish pastries, knowing that later on, Aggie would have a substantial meal ready for him.

The coffee was most stimulating after the morning's exertions and he ordered another to keep company with the second pastry. He sat on for a while after he had finished, smoking a cigarette and killing time, considering whether or not to order a third coffee. He was wishing that Juliet could have been with him here, sitting in the bay window with the pleasant sunshine pouring in. She would really have enjoyed this, he thought, with this magnificent view across the bay. He was feeling somewhat solitary, and her company would have revived his drooping spirit.

It was time to pay the bill and he left the café. He slowly walked back across the beach over the fine white sand dunes, keeping close to the sea wall as he went. The wind had picked up and was whipping up the fine sand particles above the dunes so that they were stinging into his face, and he bent over and kept more closely to the sea wall. Eventually he reached the breach in the sea wall and walked off the beach, up the slope towards the post office. Some people were entering the post office via the stone steps, but Robert went straight to Aggie's own entrance and entered the vestibule. He had brought more sand in with him on his shoes and he endeavoured to remove all traces from before going through the inner door. He entered the sanctuary of Aggie's kitchen-diner, sheltered from the incessant elements of the outside weather, sat in Aggie's armchair, selected Salmon's *West Country* from the shelves of the nearby bookcase and thumbed through it.

The next thing he knew Aggie was calling out, 'Robbie my dear, did you have a nice day?'

Robert, startled into consciousness, recollected where he was and said, 'I must have dozed off.'

'That's all right my dear, it must be the sea air – it's very tiring until you get used to it.'

Aggie had prepared a roast dinner for her and Robert. She had taken opportunities to prepare this during lulls in post office and shop activity, and now the meal was nearing completion. They sat and ate at the table not too late, and Robert recounted his experiences to her as to what he had seen during his trip around the bay.

'Yes, when we were young we used to go over to the cavern

113

for concerts. Your mother would sing up well. She has a very good voice.' Robert knew that they took part in amateur dramatics and that the old photographs they had showed the assembled cast in costume for *HMS Pinafore*, the Gilbert and Sullivan operetta, with his mother in the role of Buttercup. Her brother Jack was also there in another photograph from *The Mikado*, dressed in traditional Japanese costume, amongst many others of the family and locals. The meal was over and Robert helped Aggie clear away and wash up. They sat back and listened to the radio for a while. The 'Brains Trust', Aggie's favourite programme, was listened to by her avidly. Robert liked it also and they hung on to every word of some of the clever answers.

Simeon and John walked through the door. 'Hello Rob! How are you?' they both exclaimed.

'Hello Sim, hello John, it's grand to see you again, how are you both getting on?'

They exchanged mutual details of progress and confidences on how they were getting on in life and with their jobs and college. Aggie listened in most interestedly to all the conversation of her boys, being most happy in their company. 'John and I are going up to the Chough later for some beer, are you going to come with us, Rob?' said Simeon.

Robert leapt at the chance. 'That'll be fine, I look forward to that, boys,' said Robert.

'Meet us up at Mother's at about seven forty-five and we'll walk up together then,' said Simeon.

Simeon was always the more boisterous of the two with John being more introspective and artistic. Robert valued them equally though and loved their company. Simeon and John disappeared back to Morvah for their tea and Robert chatted on with Aggie, anticipating the evening out with the boys.

The time for the evening outing came. Robert made his good-bye to Aggie and went up to Morvah via the interconnecting corridor. He entered the hall and noticed the old dinner gong under the stairs to summons the visitors to dinner. He crossed the wood-panelled hall, opened the latch on the kitchen door, pulled back the door and entered.

Gi was at the table by the window. 'Come over and sit down,

Robert, lovely to see you,' she exclaimed. Robert went over and kissed her on the cheek. 'My, you are a handsome young man now, just like your father,' she said. 'Simeon and John will be along shortly; they're just washing, getting ready to go out, and Uncle Jack's in his workshop repairing a chair that one of the visitors broke accidentally.' Robert knew that in the season, which was quite short, the visitors took priority and they had to maximise their efforts to look after them and accommodate their every need.

Robert chatted on with Gi and gave her the latest news from home about his parents and about what he was hoping to do now that his university days were finished. Simeon and John appeared. 'My dears, you do look smart, take care now and don't drink too much up at that pub.'

The three of them took their leave of Gi and walked down the hall towards the front door of Morvah. The porch had a monk's bench either side and the front oak door opened out on to steps into a neat little courtyard garden with a fine grass lawn either side of a central paved pathway, leading to the outer door which was of similar construction to the front door. A few glass fishing floats were lying on the lawn and they attractively refracted the evening sun into its spectral colours, playing on the path edges. They closed the outer door behind them and walked up the hill in the direction of Newquay to the pub named after that extinct bird, the Cornish Chough!

When they entered the pub, Robert bought the first round. They all had pints of local bitter. He proffered cigarettes round. Simeon took one but John preferred to stick to his pipe. The evening went on convivially with their main thread of conversation centring on the good times they had together as youngsters, with the occasional conversation with some colourful local characters. At closing time, they staggered off back home entering by the main Morvah entrance. Simeon and John went straight up to bed, as they had to get up for work in the morning, and Robert managed to find his way back in the dark, down the connecting corridor to Aggie's place. He carefully eased his way through her bedroom without waking her and entered his own room. He thankfully crashed into bed and was instantly asleep.

The days Robert spent at Aggie's followed an eventful pattern for him but with large gaps of inactivity in between. This did not particularly worry him, as he knew that he probably would not get such free time to himself in the future. The next day he had decided to go for a swim and met those stomach-crashing waves out at the tideline. He noticed particularly when standing waist-deep in the water that relentless pull of the sea, and knew that this was caused by the gravitational pull of the moon. However, he could not but feel there was a hidden hand conducting the orchestra!

In the afternoon, he tried out one of Aggie's surfboards that he had taken from the vestibule. It was a long, narrow, varnished plywood board, curved up at one end. Lying himself flat on the board he occasionally caught a roller top wave and came in reasonably fast towards the beach. This was quite thrilling and the excitement only began to pall when he became so cold that he just had to leave the sea and return to the comfort of Aggie's warm kitchen.

Satisfied by his surfing exertions, he retired that afternoon to the comfortable wood-panelled lounge of Morvah and explored in depth the interesting bookcase, treating himself to a good read.

The next day, he decided to visit the village of St Columb Minor, his mother's ancestral home. He explored the church and saw the plaque commemorating his grandmother, which was donated by the family in her loving memory. She had died before Roberts' birth, and to see this had brought him closer to her memory. Later he walked back through the village and lingered outside the house that had been grandparents' and where his mother had lived as a young girl, and he allowed the nostalgia to weigh on him for a while.

On Thursday he visited the Pedlars and was invited in for tea and buns with them. He found Hector Pedlar a particularly interesting character. A true Cornishman, short and stocky, very bronzed by an inordinate amount of time spent outdoors, he had served in the war on the battleship KG5 and had many interesting tales to tell. That evening, Robert was invited to dinner with Simeon and John in Morvah. A delightful roast dinner was had and he spent another convivial evening in the lounge with them playing draughts with John, who really had mastery of the board and trounced Robert no end of times, much to Robert's annoyance!

Friday dawned and Robert was really at a loss as to what to do. Aggie said that she wanted to go to the cinema that evening in Newquay. There was a good film that she had wanted to see and she suggested that perhaps Simeon and John would want to come too. Robert said that he would order a taxi to take them down and pick them up, but Aggie insisted that it was her treat for him. It was a good A film with a mediocre B support film, and on the return, Robert and the boys dropped off at the Chough for a couple of pints before retiring for the night.

Saturday arrived and Robert was aware that Hilda was to arrive at about midday to pick him up for his return to Bodmin. He felt reluctant to return, as life was so good by the sea, but he knew that he must and more so because he was closer to seeing Juliet again.

The post office was only open until midday on Saturday and when it had closed, Aggie had more time to talk to him again whilst awaiting Hilda's arrival. They had a light lunch and then heard the car drawing up. They greeted Hilda at the door and she came in for the afternoon. Simeon and John had gone to Saturday football and had already made their goodbyes to Robert the previous evening at the pub, and so it was only necessary to say his goodbyes to Jack and Gi. Robert and Hilda did this and returned to spend the rest of the time with Aggie before their departure. Tea was had with pasties and saffron cake and splits and cream. Robert related to Hilda what he had been doing at Porth, and Hilda and Aggie talked together about mutual friends and acquaintances.

Robert made his fond farewells to Aggie and thanked her very much for looking after him. Hilda embraced her sister and they departed from Porth, with Aggie waving from her vestibule until the car had turned the corner around the post office and was on its way back to Bodmin.

Chapter Twelve

Hilda was driving the car at forty miles per hour across Goss Moor. Robert and she had been talking on and off since they had left Porth. Hilda then mentioned the fact that, tomorrow being Sunday, she had invited Juliet and her parents to Sunday lunch. They could not get down in time for church that morning so Hilda had decided to go to eight o'clock communion service and receive them later, nearer to lunchtime.

Robert was thrilled. 'That's good news, Aunt, I'll look forward to seeing her again, and of course her parents as well.'

The car sped on across Goss Moor on its approach to Bodmin. Soon the beacon was in view, dominating the town and its environs. The car sped on up Westheath Avenue and was soon within the town proper and went down Bore Street and left into Dennison Road, past the view of the old jail, continuing on and left up into Castle Hill. They garaged the car in Miss Mudge's barn, walked across the road and into the house. After nearly a week away, Robert was pleased to have returned to Bodmin, one step closer to Juliet again.

Robert awoke on the following auspicious (to him) day and was washed, dressed and down early for breakfast. Hilda had already left the house to go down to St Petroc's for the first Sunday of the month communion. It was the first Sunday of September already and Robert's proposed stay in Cornwall had one week left to run. He entered the kitchen and saw the note that Hilda had left for him propped up on the kitchen table against the sugar bowl. 'I've gone down early to St Petroc's to communion. As Alice, Leon and Juliet are coming to lunch today I won't be doing a full breakfast, so do yourself some toast and boiled eggs this morning and I'll be back as soon as possible,' read the note.

Robert was pleased to be left to his own devices and had been getting used to it during his stay at Aggie's. It gave him time to think out the possible events of the day and to recollect what had already taken place during his stay. He thought about meeting Juliet today and that it was fortuitous that his aunt had arranged it. Robert had hoped that he could still meet Juliet again later on in the week before he had to return to London, and thought that this provided him with an ideal opportunity to broach the subject. The motorbike was still in the his aunt's back yard and he would be able to use that again to visit her, before he had to return it to the AA depot at Liskeard.

Robert drank his tea and enjoyed the lightly-boiled eggs with the toast smothered in yellow Cornish butter. It had been easier to prepare on the gas stove here rather than on Aggie's coal fired range. It was a question of heat being so much easier to control on the gas cooker than on the coal fired one.

Robert had finished his breakfast, had washed up the dishes and cleared away when he heard the front door open. Hilda had returned from church. He heard her walking down the hall and then she entered the kitchen. She looked positively glowing. My word, thought Robert communion has certainly had a positive effect on her. Hilda said, 'Have you not had your breakfast, yet my dear?' noticing the fact that no dirty dishes were on show.

'Yes, Aunt,' replied Robert. 'I've had boiled eggs and toast and I did wash up.'

'That was good of you my dear, that's your good deed for the day!' she said, not quite understanding that a man might actually do that!

'How did church go, Aunt?' said Robert.

'Wonderful my dear, I feel quite resurrected, nothing like fasting and communion to make a soul realise where she is!'

Robert, who had never been a communicant, thought, she has some profound belief all right!

'Well, my dear, I will have a nice cup of tea with a piece of toast and afterwards I'll start preparing for Sunday lunch.'

Robert was told to go and sit himself down in the lounge for a while and have a read of the newspaper. He did so and lit up the inevitable cigarette, inhaling and exhaling away as he read through the *Western Morning News*. There was news of the local harvest being a bumper one for the year thanks to the fine weather, and news of the local shows and events that had also done so well this fine summer. Robert heard his aunt moving in the hall in and out of the dining room. He realised that she was probably preparing the table for lunch and so he popped his head around the lounge door and asked if he could give her a hand. The response was typical – 'No, no, my dear, I've got it all under control' – but she relented and added, 'I'll tell you what you can do though, you can decant some sherry for their arrival and arrange some glasses on the silver tray on the sideboard.'

Robert gladly accepted the job and retrieved the medium dry sherry bottle from the pantry and found an empty decanter in the bottom cupboard of the sideboard. He filled the decanter, placed it on the silver tray and arranged the set of six sherry glasses around it, checking that they were clean and shiny. He took the empty sherry bottle to the kitchen, placed it on the table and asked if she would like him to do anything else. The reply was in the negative and he was told to go back and relax in the lounge. He dutifully obeyed and was soon back behind the pages of the *Western Morning News*. The sun streamed in through the window and he was nervously keeping a watch on the church clock in anticipation of the guests' arrival. The clock started chiming twelve o'clock and he realised that they would soon be here, and the butterflies began churning in his stomach. Hilda looked in and said, 'They should arrive by one o'clock. If they arrive and I don't hear, please let them in, Robert, and pour them a sherry.'

Robert said he would and wondered if there would be any additional wine to have with the lunch other than just the sherry. They would probably get quite squiffy on the sherry anyway!

Robert heard the garden gate close. He put the newspaper hurriedly down and looked out of the window. He saw Leon and Alice walking up the path, followed by Juliet. He remained seated and waited for the formal clanging of the doorbell. He steeled himself for the encounter and moved towards the front door. Aunt Hilda must have heard the bell but she was obviously leaving the initial meeting to him. Robert opened the door and Leon shook him warmly by the hand. 'Good to see you again, my boy. We parked up by the police station, easiest spot to leave the car rather than on this hill.'

Robert greeted Alice. 'Go on through into the lounge and Aunt will be through shortly.' He then saw Juliet and she moved warmly towards him, and their hands met and clasped together.

'Did you enjoy your stay by the sea, Robert?'

'Yes,' he replied, 'but it would have been nicer if you had been with me.'

She smiled at him, and it was then that Robert noticed that she looked a little tired and drawn. It was probably due to all the hard work during the harvesting that had just been completed, he thought. They walked through into the lounge. Leon and Alice were seated in the two armchairs either side of the fireplace and Robert directed Juliet to sit on the prayer chair over by the window. Robert took a straight-backed chair facing the window, and the church clock chimed the singular one o'clock stroke.

Alice broke the silence. 'I told Hilda that we'd be here by one o'clock and here we be, but where is she?'

Everybody laughed and Robert said that she would soon be through when she had completed lunch preparations. In the meantime, he had been instructed to ply them with sherry! At this they all laughed again. Robert brought in the large, full sherry glasses and they all sipped and chatted away, the conversation growing more animated with the consumption of the sherry. Hilda walked into the room, having tidied herself up from her kitchen attire, and greeted them, with, 'Hello my dears all, I'm so glad that you could come today. It must be nice to get away after all that harvesting!'

Alice responded, 'Oh, it's a pleasure, Hilda maid, to get away from the farm for a bit.'

Leon did not say anything to this but toyed with his pipe and grinned over to Robert and Juliet. He said, 'Well what do you think, Anne my dear, would you rather be down here with Robert now or back up on the farm for the moment?'

Juliet blushed and looked down and did not answer. Robert sensed her embarrassment and tried to change the subject, but Hilda broke in and said, sipping her sherry, 'Let's go through to the dining room now, or lunch will be getting cold.'

She led the way and said, 'Seat yourselves down now, Jul— Anne, over by the window, Leon and Robert either side of her and Alice and myself near the door.' The tureens of vegetables were steaming on the table and Hilda, followed by Alice, went to the kitchen to bring in the plates of roast beef and Yorkshire pudding that were placed at each table setting. 'Now, my dears, help yourselves to roast potatoes and to the carrots and runner beans. All home-grown, from local gardens,' she was at pains to point out.

After they had helped themselves liberally from the gravy boat and from the horseradish sauce bowl, they tucked in to their respective lunches. The cutlery was the best solid silver and was a pleasure to use, and the beef was mouth watering and the beans exceptionally tender. They all relished the food and Leon turned to Alice and said, 'Well, my dear, I've now found a cook to equal you.'

Alice chuckled and said, 'Now, now, Leon, you know that Hilda has always been an exceptionally dab hand at cooking. Brought up properly, she was.'

Hilda chuckled at this. Robert got up and refilled the sherry glasses. Whilst perhaps sherry was not the prescribed drink for this meal, it was nevertheless going down a treat. While the conversation buzzed at the table, Robert had the opportunity to talk quietly to Juliet for a moment away from the main conversational thrust. 'Yes, I did miss you whilst I was down at Porth, and it would have been wonderful if you could have been with me.'

'I would have liked that Robert, I have never been that way and I understand it is a beautiful stretch of coast.'

'Oh yes, it definitely is, you would have to go a long way to find anything finer. A bit of sea air would have brought out the colour in your cheeks,' he continued, referring obliquely to her somewhat pale look at the moment.

She sensed that he had noticed and countered with the fact that she looked that way at the moment because of all the hard work bringing in the harvest. She did not expand further on this but changed the subject as quickly as possible. Robert said that he was staying with Hilda for almost another week and he would like to meet up with her again before going back to London. She agreed that Thursday evening would be the best time and said that she understood that it would be the motorbike again!

The roast beef had been eaten by now, and Hilda and Alice busied themselves clearing the table. The pudding was the old favourite of hot apple pie and blackberries topped with clotted cream that just melted into every crevice of the pie. They ate with pleasure and the church clock stuck two thirty.

'The afternoon is getting on,' exclaimed Hilda. She directed them to leave all the empty dishes on the table and retire to the lounge for coffee. They returned there retaking their original seats whilst Hilda brought in the coffee pot and cups on the tray, and placed it the small gate-leg table that she had situated in the middle of the room.

'Good coffee, Aunt,' said Robert.

'Yes my dear, I bought it at Jack Bray's, he does stock the best blends and knows his coffee sources.'

They all agreed that it was fine coffee and the afternoon's conversation continued on a light amicable note.

Robert stood up a while later and said, 'I'll stretch my legs for a bit.' Turning to Juliet, he said, 'Will you come with me?'

She stood up and they walked out through the hall to the front garden. Alice looked across at Hilda and said, 'They seem to be getting along fine, those two, but I don't know what will become of it!'

Hilda responded to Alice, 'Oh, it's lovely to see them together.'

Leon remained his usual quiet self, but thought deeply on the matter.

Robert and Juliet walked slowly around the garden, unaware of its size or plants as they were deeply absorbed in one another. Their bare arms, her in a summer dress and him in a short-sleeved shirt, touched as they walked closely, and it seemed as though there would be no end to this blissful encounter. Tired of wandering around the garden they sat together on the granite steps to the front door of the house and watched the late summer sun playing on the rocks and making the mica impurities glisten. She almost rested her head on his shoulder, and he almost embraced her, being in such proximity side by side, but they resisted for the sake of form under the circumstances and thought perhaps to reserve that for a later date.

They sat there almost in a dreamlike slumber in the warm sunshine, wishing for it not to end.

Hilda interrupted their idyll and called to them, 'Come in my dears for some tea, it'll be getting colder now as the evening draws in.'

They reluctantly stretched themselves up and returned. Leon was puffing away at his pipe and Alice was sipping tea from Hilda's best china, Royal Doulton. Hilda was pouring tea and handed a cup to Juliet and one to Robert as they entered. 'Sit yourselves down, my dears,' she said.

'What have you two been up to then?' enquired Alice.

It was a shame to break the spell, thought Robert, and then Juliet said, 'Talking, Mother, just talking together about our lives.'

The answer was so definitive that no further question could be asked on the subject and so Alice turned to Leon and said, 'I think we'll have to be getting back soon to give a hand to the boys to bed down the animals.'

'Oh, I think they can handle them all right on their own,' responded Leon, who was quite comfortable in his chair with his pipe and cup of tea.

They talked on for a while longer, eating cake and drinking more tea, until Leon decided that it was time to be getting back after all. 'Well, Hilda, you have done us proud today. A most wonderful lunch and tea, and most agreeable company, don't you think, Robert?'

Robert responded, 'Absolutely, couldn't have been better – thank you, Aunt,' thinking that the best thing that afternoon was his meeting with Juliet.

The Mentreaths prepared to get going and Hilda led them out by the back door. They walked past the motorbike and Leon said, 'You be careful on that bike, particularly if you take my daughter out on it again.'

Robert said he would, and would be looking for his own car in due course when he was in employment. He said he would walk them up to their car whilst Hilda made her goodbyes at the back gate, to save her leg from walking up the hill. They reached the car on the flat ground, by the police station and Robert leaned over the wall and patted the tortoise on the back. 'Look, Juliet,' he said, 'here's the tortoise close to the wall.'

She leaned over as well and patted the tortoise. 'The tortoise is still here, then,' she said. 'I have not really seen it since I was a child.'

Then they both giggled childishly and turned back to the car. Robert shook Leon's hand and kissed Alice on the cheek. Leon got into the driver's seat and Alice sat beside him. Robert opened the door for Juliet and helped her into the back, and bent over and kissed her full on the lips as she went in. She responded with ardour but, realising where she was, broke off and sat down. Leon and Alice had not noticed this kiss. Before closing the door on Juliet, Robert said, 'Look forward to seeing you on Thursday.'

'Yes Robert, me too.'

He closed the door, the engine started and the car moved off in the direction of the moor. Robert waved them off. He walked back to Hilda's, a contented man, thinking that he and Juliet were now really becoming a couple!

Chapter Thirteen

Robert awoke early the next day and immediately the events of yesterday poured through his mind. How successful it had all been. He and Juliet had got on wonderfully. Any of the initial reserve had been erased by a growing natural harmony together, and he felt so comfortable in her presence. This was a good sign as far as he was concerned, as it took a special young woman for Robert to feel that comfortable with! The only thing that bothered him was that initially she had looked so pale and drawn, and he hoped that she was not ailing for something. It crossed his mind that it may well have been down to some form of 'women's complaint' and thereafter dismissed it from his mind, not of course being an expert on such matters!

A knocking came at the door and Robert shouted out, 'Come in.'

Hilda opened the door and limped through in her characteristic manner with the rattling tea tray, but this time she had a greater sense of urgency about her. 'Robert my dear, here is a telegram for you. The boy did not wait for a reply but if you need to, you can go down to the post office later this morning.' He sat up sharply and took the yellow telegram envelope from her hand, and with a degree of trepidation ripped it open and rapidly scanned the contents. It read: RETURN HOME IMMEDIATELY STOP JOB OFFER AND INTERVIEW AVAILABLE STOP AEI STOP DAD. Hilda waited and then said, 'Nothing serious, I hope my dear?'

'No, Aunt,' replied Robert, 'but I'll have to disappoint you and return home early as there is a job offer for me which I really cannot miss.' Prior to journeying to Cornwall, Robert had been seen by one or two companies as a prospective graduate employee and AEI (Amalgamated Engineering Industries), that prestigious British company, had obviously come up trumps!

'Oh my dear, that *is* good for you, but I'm sorry that you'll be going back immediately.'

'Well, Aunt, I suppose that I had better arrange the train journey back for tomorrow. I'll go to the post office later to send a reply to this telegram to Mum and Dad, to tell them to expect me tomorrow, and then I will go to the town station to book the return journey. I will have to write a letter to Juliet telling her of the change of plan, as we had arranged to meet on Thursday.' The fact that Robert had now to leave Juliet without a further meeting came as a blow to him, but what else could he do? He had to obtain good employment; that was vital to his future. But he would keep in touch with Juliet via letters and would get down here again as soon as possible to see her. He knew that she would understand the situation and perhaps in time he might obtain some employment down here, even in Plymouth perhaps.

Hilda walked out of the room and Robert attended to the tea and biscuits and downed them quite rapidly. He got up, washed and dressed rapidly and was soon down to breakfast. Hilda had the smoking frying pan on the go and Robert was presented with the enormous hogs pudding fried breakfast. I'll miss these when I go back to London, he thought to himself. That was not all he would miss – he would miss this house, his aunt and the atmosphere in this house, but most of all he would miss Juliet, he pondered. Yet there was nothing for it but to take his fate and live with it.

With breakfast finished and with a brief moment in the lounge for a cigarette and a read of the newspaper, Robert was ready for his walk into town. He suddenly remembered the motorbike. I'll have to get it back to Liskeard this afternoon, he thought. Mr Burton was good enough to lend it to me and I must get it back to him without fail before the day is out, he mused.

Robert walked down town past St Petroc's, past the everflowing spring at the steps and over to St Nicholas Street on the way to Bodmin Town Station. He reached the station and all was quiet. No trains were in, they had departed much earlier. He went in to the ticket office and arranged to have his return ticket transferred to the London Express leaving at nine o'clock the next morning. On leaving the station he wandered further up the road towards the DCLI barracks and the soldiers' statue. The Military Museum was just here but he had no time to visit now. He had been in there before when he was younger, and had been suitably impressed, as all boys were, with the military exploits of the regiment and how it had developed over the centuries. He turned and retraced his steps back past the town station and on to the post office to send the reply telegram to inform his parents of his return. Entering the post office, it was all neat and formal and the counter girl was very polite. He wrote out his message, which was checked by the girl to confirm that it was exactly as he wanted it, before its transcription on to the tape ribbon. It was 4d a word, so one minimised the words to keep the cost down. All Robert said was: WILL RETURN TUESDAY STOP NINE A.M. TRAIN TO PADDINGTON STOP ROBERT. Robert paid the fee and left the post office, and returned to Castle Hill. Hilda insisted that he had lunch before returning the motorbike, so Robert had to acquiesce. The lunch was good though – a stew with dumplings followed by peaches and clotted cream. They talked on about how well things had gone with the visit of yesterday and about how Robert should come down again as soon as possible after getting settled in employment.

The lunch over, Robert was anxious to be getting the motorbike back to Liskeard as soon as possible, so he made to go but Hilda insisted that he let his lunch go down properly before driving off. At that moment, Miss Mudge emerged with her cows and proceeded to drive them up the hill. Hilda chuckled. 'My, she is later than ever today, I don't know how she makes a living over there.'

Robert observed her going past the window and wondered how many more times he would see this event occurring. Miss Mudge and her bovines had now passed by and Robert said, 'I really must get that bike back now.'

Hilda said, 'Take care then, I'll see you about tea time. If you do see Mr Burton, ask him to call sometime when he is down this way again.'

Robert straddled the bike and kick-started it. It did not start immediately and it took a few kicks and timing adjustments before the engine was ticking over nicely. He eased the bike out across the pavement on to the road in first gear and was soon down the hill around St Petroc's, on the road to Liskeard. He reached the AA depot, remembering the route from his first visit, but nobody was around. No AA patrolmen and no girl in the office. They were probably still out to lunch. There was nothing for it but to park up the bike, write a hurried note, wrap the keys in it and drop them through the letterbox. Now, thought Robert, how do I get back?

There were three possibilities: taxi, bus or hitch a lift. Robert had not really considered the last as a viable option, but as he walked out on to the main road he saw a lorry approaching and instinctively thumbed for a lift. He was amazed when the lorry slowed down and came to a halt on the grass verge. He ran up past the load of straw bales to the cab. A grizzled, unshaven face surmounted by a cloth cap looked down at him and said, 'Where to, squire?'

'Bodmin, please,' responded Robert.

''Ess, I'll drop 'ee off there then.'

Robert climbed into the passenger side of the cab. The seat was covered in an old worn blanket, the leather was decaying and split, and the cab floor was liberally sprinkled with straw. The lorry drove off and Robert tried to draw the driver into conversation but to no avail, apart from a few grunts and long drawn out ''Esses'. In no time, the lorry slammed to a halt and the words came, 'Bodmin, then.' Robert made his thanks and climbed down. The lorry crashed into gear and lurched on its way. That was a mystery, thought Robert, I really don't know where that man came from or where he was going, but nevertheless I'm thankful for the lift. He walked back into the house, recounted to his aunt his small adventure and retired to his room to gather his things together for his departure tomorrow.

That afternoon, he sat at the great desk in the dining room and proceeded to write a letter to Juliet, to explain the situation of his sudden departure to her and to reassure her of his regard for her and that he would write often and would hope to return to Bodmin as soon as possible after he had settled and made a good start in his work. He gave her his London address in the letter so she could reply. Later in the afternoon he walked back to the post office to buy some stamps and post the letter to Juliet. Feeling satisfied he had done all he could, he returned to the house and spent the remainder of the afternoon in the company of his aunt in the lounge, enjoying the sun that streamed in through the window and exchanging pleasantries over cups of tea.

Tuesday morning arrived. Robert was up early with his grip packed and resting in the hall. His raincoat was draped across it ready for use, as the weather was on the change into rain. Hilda was up early too, insisting that she take Robert to the station to see him off, but he had insisted that it was not necessary as the town station was only down the road and easy to walk to. They breakfasted, Robert on the big fry-up 'that would sustain him for the journey' and Hilda more lightly on a poached egg.

Robert was to leave the house no later than eight thirty that morning, and as that time drew near he thanked Hilda profoundly for such a wonderful stay and for looking after him so well. He presented her with a bottle of cream sherry and said that when she saw Juliet, Leon and Alice again, to give them his love and added that he would be communicating with Juliet by letter. She understood this and tearfully embraced Robert on the steps in the front of the house. It was raining now and Robert had his raincoat on with the collar pulled up, grip in hand, ready for a rapid dash to the town station. He turned to wave goodbye to Hilda, who was standing on the steps, and the thought crossed his mind as to whether he would see her again. She was looking older now. He closed his mind to the thought and said to himself, Yes, of course I will, but he was not fully convinced. He reached the garden gate, opened it, turned and made a last goodbye wave. He walked through and the gate slammed loudly shut behind him.

He walked rapidly past St Petroc's, past the spring that still gurgled even in the rain and quickly on to the town station. He reached it at a quarter to nine, which gave him plenty of time to have his ticket checked and to find a suitable carriage. He found a deserted compartment and sat by the window, facing the engine, after having thrown his grip in the overhead luggage rack. All was quiet apart from the hissing of steam issuing from the engine, and the passengers were extremely scarce. Undoubtedly it would start to fill up further down the line around Plymouth, he suspected. He lit a cigarette and waited for the train to pull out. All in all, it had been a good holiday for him. The best part by far was, of course, having met Juliet.

The journey back was totally different to the journey down. Its tedium was only relieved by the occasional good view through the misty rain, and the lunch was good, but eating alone without Juliet was not quite the same. The train sped, on picking up more passengers at Plymouth and of course crossing Brunel's bridge again and the Dawlish run was as awe-inspiring as usual. The compartment became full with passengers as the journey progressed and Robert delved into a paperback detective story he had bought at Bricknells, as a way of ignoring the other passengers and passing the time. The train drew into the London suburbs and the smokiness of it all became apparent – not quite so clean as the West Country. The train slowed down to a crawl on its approach into Paddington Station and came to a halt with the engine still emitting steam, which hissed away as its pressure level reduced.

Robert alighted on to a fairly deserted platform. The announcements were blaring out hollowly and echoing around the station hall as they urgently announced various imminent departures. Engines were steaming and emitting occasional ear-piercing blasts. It all seemed a very surreal scene, and then Robert saw his father standing there. A long grey overcoat and a trilby pulled down over his eyes almost characterised him as a character in the detective story he had just been reading. He greeted his father and they shook hands. 'I've got a taxi waiting, boy,' Robert's father said. 'Thought that we'd get home quicker this way than by taking the tube and bus.'

His father, Percy, led the way out into the station yard to the waiting taxi.

Chapter Fourteen

Robert was pleased to be back in his London home. It was good to be with his parents again. He had not gone directly back there after he finished at university, because he had so wanted to get away from London to the West Country after that arduous last term. This was no slight to his parents but had demonstrated in a sense the family solidarity, with relatives who were only too eager to help. Back home now he was pleased to be settled for a while at least in the comfortable three-bed semi in the attractive Cricklewood suburb of north-west London. His parents had moved there before the war when it had been newly built, and now it was attractively mature without decline. His father was not a particularly ambitious man and he and his mother were content with their situation, although some of their neighbours and good friends had moved on to slightly more salubrious districts nearby.

His mother was of course so pleased to have him back home again. Very much like her sisters, she doted on the menfolk, and Robert being her son could do no wrong. Robert did at times find her attentions somewhat overbearing and knew that in due course, now he was to start work, he would have to move away to find his own accommodation. But for the moment he was content to be looked after! His father by contrast to his mother was a very quiet man and would allow one to have one's freedom, but with occasional good words of advice to keep a lad on the 'correct path'.

The area had not been subjected to any severe wartime bombing as it was certainly out of the blitz area of London, but a nearby railway marshalling yard and aircraft factory had been targeted, albeit not particularly successfully. So in this area you did not have as much post-war damage still waiting to be repaired as you did in the centre of London.

They were sitting in the dining room looking out through the French windows into the attractive, small garden. Robert remembered when the windows had the crossed tapes on them to prevent flying glass from any nearby bomb blasts. That did not happen, and those years had now passed and they were on to that promising new post-war era of technology advances and suchlike. His mother, Winnie, was anxious to glean from Robert all that had happened in Cornwall and find out how her sisters were getting on and how they were currently looking. His father listened impassively until he found his opportunity to proffer the letter in front of Robert that had invited him to interview at AEI. The interview was on Friday. It was currently Wednesday, and Robert was pleased that he had some time before he had to attend. Time to recollect his thoughts! It more or less said that from their graduate recruitment drive at the university they had selected Robert for his potential on a new project that was of great importance to the security of the nation and for the future of the company! The interview would take place at Stanmore – that was only about ten miles away. It was very convenient as tube and bus links were numerous and nearby.

Robert spent Thursday pottering about. He tried out his suit to see if it still fitted him. It did, although it was a trifle snug at the waistline, which he had to put down to all those cooked breakfasts at his aunt's and all the other heavy meals. It did however fit well enough, and a good brush down had it looking as good as new. His mother fussed around ironing a white shirt for him and he selected a suitably sober tie to go with the suit.

He went down to the local shops for cigarettes and for some grocery items for his mother. On his return to the house he saw Mrs Darling in her front garden, and she was pleased to see him and to welcome him back. He enquired after her daughter Angela and how had she been getting on in her nursing career. Mrs Darling was widowed and was living on a good pension bequeathed to her from her husband's company, a meat importer. They had spent some time in Argentina working for the company and her descriptions of it sounded so exotic. He returned to his parents house and looked across to the house where a childhood chum of his, David, used to live. The family had moved on to Watford. The father, a printer, had moved the family closer to Oldham's press, where he worked. Robert wondered how David was getting on. He had not seen him for a few years, although Robert's mother had kept in touch with David's mother. Robert closed the garden gate and entered the house. His thoughts turned to Juliet and he decided that he would write her a letter telling her all that had happened since his return to London. He struggled a bit, as the quantity of news was not great, but he did express his regret again for having to leave early without seeing her once more, and added that after he was settled in work he would take the earliest opportunity to go and see her again on the moor. He promised that he would write again and tell her about his job in due course.

Later, Robert and his mother were sitting in the lounge relaxing and chatting when they heard the garden gate slam shut and then the front door open. His father had arrived back from the office, and he entered the room carrying his *Evening Standard*. Percy sat down in a chair and said, 'Phew that was a journey I'm glad to be rid of. Those tubes are getting more tightly packed than ever.'

His father worked for an insurance company and by a series of buses and tubes he managed to get to and from the office, situated closer to central London than their home.

'I'll get you a nice cup of tea then, Percy,' said Robert's mother. 'That'll be lovely, Win.'

Percy lit a cigarette and offered one to Robert. 'Thanks, Dad.' They both lit up and puffed smoke profusely around the room.

Later, they moved to the dining room and a dinner of lamb chops, potatoes, carrots and cabbage was eaten, followed by treacle pudding and custard. With the meal and dishes cleared away, they settled down to listen to a couple of radio shows on the 'Light Programme' for the evening. Robert relaxed, but flowing through his mind were all the possibilities of questions that might be asked at the AEI interview tomorrow. He even had some of his college notes on his lap, which he flicked through to remind himself of some academic points and other things.

Friday dawned and Robert was up, breakfasted and dressed in his suit in good time. He carefully brought the knot of his tie together in the crevice of the stiff white collar he was wearing, so that it had a formal but rakish look. His father said, 'To get there then, you will have to catch the tube at Golders Green, get the Northern Line and go through four stops until you get out at Edgware. From there catch the 229 bus to Stanmore.'

His father knew the area quite well, as he had been stationed at the RAF headquarters at Stanmore during the war, although he did not know the exact location of AEI, but it was a fairly prominent building according to all accounts. His mother and father wished him luck and told him not to be nervous during the interview and to speak up well.

Robert left the house and made his way down to Golders Green tube station. The journey was short and was followed by a short bus journey. He had to ask the exact location of AEI from a local newsagent, and was pointed in the correct direction. Arriving by foot at the main gate, he was greeted by a commissionaire, dressed in a smart blue uniform with golden sergeant's stripes, wearing war ribbons on his chest. He was directed to the interview office area and a female secretary took his details and asked him to sit down in the waiting room. She said 'Mr Hicks-Arnot will be with you shortly, would you like a coffee whilst you wait?'

'Yes please,' replied Robert, as by now his mouth and throat were particularly dry.

Hicks-Arnot walked in and introductions were made. 'I'm Frank, and you must be…'

'Robert,' blurted out Robert.

'I shall call you Bob, then,' responded Hicks-Arnot. Thereafter Robert's name at work, 'Bob', stuck with him always. 'Come on through to the boardroom; we'll have a quiet chat there,' said Hicks-Arnot.

The boardroom was impressive, wood-panelled, and a large, highly-polished table dominated the centre of the room. Pictures of warships and aircraft covered the walls. Robert observed Hicks-Arnot. He was a well-built man with greying, swept-back hair and a goatee beard. He had a generous tummy area over which was stretched a colourful waistcoat. He wore a large, checked sports jacket with leather elbow pads. A spotted handkerchief hung out of the top pocket of his jacket and a large woollen tie hung loosely around his neck. He appeared to be a most genial character. They sat at one end of the table and Frank signalled to the secretary for more coffee and biscuits.

'I'll come straight to the point. We've got to get a new guided weapon system into service with the navy within the next ten years or sooner.'

'Oh,' said Robert, 'I was not aware that the they had any in service yet,' remembering the old battleships laid up in the Devonport creeks.

'Well,' said Frank, 'yes and no. We've been developing them since the end of the war, but not very successfully. Some are just about to go into service, being bolted to some old warships, but they are really out of date before they get into service. The Americans have had their own problems but they are still streaks ahead of us and we must have something new to counter the Soviet threat against us, to protect our fleet.'

Robert was not particularly aware of the Soviet threat but picked up on the urgency in Frank's voice.

'Judging by your academic results, we think that you are the man to fit in with this project. We need a person who can understand the mathematical implications of the radar reflections and how they will be perceived by the missile guidance system.'

Robert thought nervously that yes, he had done rather well at the electromagnetic wave theory, but it had taken him a lot of hard work to come to terms with it.

Frank went on. 'The guidance unit needs a complete revamp as well. We've already gone to miniature valves, but they still consume too much power and we are doing a pilot study on going to transistors. You could help out there also.'

Robert just knew about transistors although his university course had not included them. He knew the term 'transfer resistor' had been truncated into 'transistor' and that they had an amplifying effect based on this property and worked on an electrical current low voltage basis rather than a high voltage basis. Their main advantage seemed to be their low power usage and their light weight, well suited to an in-flight missile. Frank broke in to Robert's thoughts. 'Don't worry about not being an expert in transistors – we've got plenty of blokes who are coming up to speed on that, and you can always learn from them. I'm a valve man myself and I don't understand these damned transistors,' he said. He went on to explain his interest in amateur radio and his development of valve circuits and the fact that he had managed a wartime factory manufacturing radio valves for RAF sets.

They talked on and Frank finally said, 'We want you, Bob, what do you say?'

Robert was silent for a moment and then said, 'Yes it sounds very interesting and exciting, I'll accept.'

'Well done, old boy,' said Frank, and vigorously shook him by the hand. 'I reckon a salary of around £1,000 per year will be in order and I'll get your papers etc sorted out by the personnel department.'

'That's very good,' said Robert, somewhat bemused by the rapid turn of events and the sudden prospect of a flow of income. 'Do you mind if I smoke?' he said to Frank and offered him a Players cigarette.

'Go ahead, old boy,' came the reply, 'but I'm a pipe man,' and he clamped a curly pipe firmly between his teeth. 'Can you start as soon as possible? Next Monday would be ideal.'

Robert had not anticipated such an early start from the interview, but accepted.

'We'll make sure the paperwork is done concurrently with you starting work. It normally takes a bit longer, but under the circumstances we can force it through,' said Frank.

On saying goodbye to him, Frank mentioned that the first couple of days would be fairly easy going, getting to know the other engineers. He would give Robert a tour around the offices, labs, drawing office and factory area.

Robert returned home reeling somewhat from his rapid injection into the world of work. It would take a little while to get used to after years of academic study, and he hoped that he would have the energy to keep up all the effort it would undoubtedly require. The pay, of course, would make all the difference; he might even be able to afford that car he knew he needed.

His parents were very pleased with his good news but somewhat surprised with the rapid start. His mother had been hoping that he might have been around home for a while longer before beginning work. Well, there was a weekend before starting and that would undoubtedly be a time for enjoyment!

The weekend went by in rather a phoney war atmosphere – knowing that something was going to happen, but not just yet. It passed with Robert enjoying the company of his parents to the full. The early September weather was still fine and they sat out in deckchairs in the garden, enjoying the sun.

Monday morning arrived and Robert dressed down somewhat from his interview suit, taking the tip from Frank in wearing a sports jacket and casual trousers, with a white shirt and striped tie.

He arrived at the AEI entrance and noticed that the building was in the art deco style – well, it had to be, having been built in the thirties! It was an impressive-looking building and the style of it was to Robert's taste. He was met at reception by Frank with a hearty, 'Hello, Bob,' and was taken through to his office for coffee. Frank was the Company Chief Engineer. All projects were ultimately under his control and it was one of his functions to allocate resources to particular projects. Robert was one of these resources.

They drank their coffee, with Frank telling Bob of his week-end spent in his Radio Ham attic, contacting various Hams around the country and overseas. He said that one day perhaps Bob would pop round to his home in Dollis Hill and listen in with him when he was 'doing the rounds'. His wife, Marion, would be pleased to meet him and they could have an evening drink together.

The coffee was finished and it was time to meet the project team. Frank led Robert down the corridor to the office lab area. It was an open-plan desk area with surrounding benches carrying electronic equipments. Glass-partitioned offices surrounded the open-plan area, looking out on to a paved courtyard with a grassed central area with a shrubbery border.

Frank took Robert into the first office next to the door and bellowed out, 'Hello Ben, here's Bob who I've been telling you about, soon to become your expert on Sea Streak.'

Ben looked up from his desk, still clutching his slide rule. 'I hope he'll be better than the last expert I had, then,' and grinned.

'Yes,' said Frank, 'we don't talk about him now, do we, having done a runner on us and going over to the States.' Ben and Robert shook hands. 'Ben's the Sea Streak project leader. I'll leave you in his capable hands. He'll tell you everything you want to know about the project.'

With that, Frank withdrew and returned to his own office. Ben launched into more detail on the missile and why its projected design was superior to other types. It was not a slow Beam Rider that had to sit in a radar beam illuminating an aircraft target, but it had much faster Ramjet engine and tracked the enemy plane in angle and velocity, receiving the reflected radar waves from the target, calculating and predicting its future position from that data. It was to be a fleet area protection weapon, and AEI also hoped to develop it into an anti-missile version. It was vital that the Royal Navy came up to date with this modern weapon system.

'This is where you come in, Bob – we have to perfect the guidance unit. We have all the facilities you will need here and it will be necessary to attend flight trials down at the Aberporth range and also at the Pendine rocket range in Wales, as often as required.'

Robert asked various questions, realising that this could be a hard haul. He was then taken out to meet some of the project's team immediately outside in the lab. He was introduced to Brian Beverly-Smythe (known to his friends as BBS) and to Dave Watling (known as What-Ho!), both experienced electronic engineers but struggling somewhat with the conversion to the transistor technology. There were huge quantities of paperwork and technical handbooks stacked on the bookshelves.

He was taken by Ben to see the massive drawing office, with its rows and rows of drawing boards and draughtsmen, and was introduced to the team directly responsible for drawing up all the Sea Streak configurations. Ben took him on to the test and tuning area and the antenna range, and introduced him to the engineers and technicians there and then on to the trials team area, with those stalwarts who organised the particular trials requirements and mustered the equipments and test boxes.

Ben then took him back to the lab and to the desk allocated for his use, and gave him some background reading material for the project. He spent the rest of the day at his desk reading, breaking off for lunch in the subsidised canteen. He joined Brian and Dave at a table and had steak and kidney pie, chips and beans, followed by roly-poly pudding.

It was a long, tiring day, what with all the new things he had to pick up on, but he had already formulated an approach for his future work there. He unloaded most of the contents from his briefcase into his desk, including a slide rule, some log tables and mathematic and electronics notes from his college days, and was pleased when five o'clock came and he could make the return journey home. Tomorrow would be another day, he thought as he walked out, past those clocking out, to the waiting bus.

Chapter Fifteen

Robert had been working at AEI now for six months and was beginning to feel an inexorable desire to get away for a break. The work had been hard and unrelenting as witnessed by his desk strewn with papers and his bookcase overflowing with documents and product data books. His ashtray was always full to overbrimming and coffee cup circles were in evidence at the corner of his desk. He had been to the Aberporth trials three times now and every trial produced a new problem, seemingly irresolvable, but always having a solution or a development enhancement.

It was not that Ben was a slave-driver but he had his schedules to keep. Frank had his and the Ministry had theirs, expecting perfect results every time. It was impossible to produce these perfect results but the Ministry did not seem to be aware of this and they just applied the greater pressure of their expectations. 'The RN needs this missile – it is vital to national security,' came the clarion cry. Every change was an effort and all the engineers stayed on well beyond normal working hours in order to complete their tasks.

Robert was smoking heavily now and it was beginning to have an effect on his health. He noticed a certain breathlessness and any physical exertion had become a greater effort for him. He thought that he really must cut down on the cigarettes but they had a beneficial effect in that they enabled him to concentrate on the painstaking technical work he had to perform. During this period, he had letters from Juliet that cheered him and gave him an incentive to carry on during this difficult, busy time. Juliet had been pleased to receive his letters and was amused at his description of the characters he had to work with, but she was somewhat appalled at the workload he had currently to put up with. Although she did write, 'It's like farming you are never without something to do!'

He was soon made a senior engineer and, in keeping with his

higher status, had two engineers working for him, more autonomy with visits and his own direct telephone line. He received many calls on this from Ministry officials and from sub-contractors, and it did allow him on occasions to receive private calls. Most of them were usually local and you still had to get permission for any long-distance calls. One particularly harrowing day he received a call from his old college friend Charles. They had lost contact for a while but Charles had traced him through the grapevine and suggested they meet up again. Robert was pleased with this contact and asked Charles how his family was and how their mutual friend, George, was getting along. Charles and George were friends before Robert had met them and they were both employed by the Decca Radar Company at Tolworth.

Charles said that George was getting along famously and he was now engaged to the girl he had met during his college days. The invite however was specifically to Robert, to join Charles for the weekend at his parental home in Reigate. Robert accepted without reservation. 'That'll be grand, Charles, I could do with a break. I'll be down Friday evening after work,' he said.

That was thus arranged and Robert's spirits soared. It would do him good to get away. He now had a car – an old Ford – but it was quite capable of doing what he wanted in the way of travelling. Charles had always had sports cars, but Robert found them too low down on the road and rather short on legroom for him as well as the general lack of storage space.

Robert told his parents on his return home that evening and his mother was pleased that Charles had made contact with him again, a boy who she had a real liking for. 'He comes from a good family,' she said. 'He's certainly a fine quality friend.'

The working week continued for Robert at a relentless pace and he breathed a sigh of relief when Friday afternoon came around. He was hoping for a quick get away and he already had his grip packed with his weekend clothes in the boot of the car. Others too had similar ideas for that weekend. Frank wanted to get away early for a gathering of Radio Hams and Ben was off to the south coast for some sailing. So Robert felt in good company when it came to five o'clock that afternoon and he exited the company premises as rapidly as the rest. He was in his car and out of the car park in no time at all, and was soon on his way to south London, through Westminster on to Wandsworth, towards Sutton and then to Reigate. He generally had a rough look at the map before moving off, memorising the main towns on the way, and then followed the road signs in their direction until arrival at the destination.

Driving into Reigate on the A25 he soon found the turning into Briarsfield road and halted the car just outside number twenty-seven. The house was Victorian and situated high above the road, with steps leading up to it. Spacious with many rooms, it had a rambling quality with quiet areas for study and for reading. Charles' father was an English academic with an enormous library of books, and Robert on previous occasions had perused his bookshelves and was very impressed with their enormous range.

Robert rang the doorbell and the door was opened by Charles. 'Bob, great to see you,' and they shook hands, grinning at one another at their reunion. 'I thought we had lost touch after college. It was such a mad scramble after the finals that I think everybody just ran off home in a hurry without making proper arrangements.'

'Yes, I know,' replied Robert, 'but I'm glad you contacted me again Charles.' They went into the house towards the lounge, talking and reminiscing on college days and friends.

'I am still in contact with George at Decca's and we can arrange to meet up with him soon,' said Charles.

They continued talking of college days and of their more recent work experiences. Coincidently, Charles was working on the development of navigational radar for naval ships, but it had no relationship to the missile project that Robert was working on.

They were sitting in the lounge overlooking the large rear garden when Patricia, Charles's younger sister, walked in. 'Bobby,' she exclaimed. 'How lovely to see you again,' she cooed, and looked at him with admiration. Robert thought that she had a bit of a soft spot for him but did not encourage it as she was Charles's sister and she did have a boyfriend, Neal! What she saw in Neal was a bit of a mystery to Robert but nevertheless they seemed to be well suited.

Charles's mother came into the room later and said, 'Bob, so lovely to see you again. You are looking well.'

Robert stood up and shook her hand and he thanked her very much for the invite to stay with them. She brought some tea in and they sat and chatted for a while. Robert told them of his recent adventures in Cornwall and of his meeting with Juliet. 'Sounds to me like there will be a wedding before too long,' said Mrs Preston, Charles's mother.

She was interested to hear of the farm on Bodmin moor and Pat was too. They both liked aspects of farming and dealing with animals and perhaps one day they might venture to engage in such activities themselves!

Later on, Mr Preston, Charles's father, came in having just returned from the college where he taught. Robert shook hands with him and was interested in listening to his latest research in the old English language. Robert admired Mr Preston's incredible knowledge of his pet subject but realised that Mr Preston's admiration for modern engineering developments was somewhat muted.

As the evening drew on, dinner was laid on the kitchen table that served well enough as a convenient dining area. Robert sat at the table with the family and Mr Preston paused to say grace before eating. This was an embarrassing moment for Robert as he normally did not say grace before meals. He looked down fixedly at his plate whilst the family crossed themselves and Mr Preston said the thanksgiving prayers. They were a catholic family but Charles did not particularly show great evidence of his faith generally and Robert assumed that Charles's practice of his faith was at a low ebb, no doubt influenced by the increasing secularisation of society. Robert did admire nevertheless this expression of faith and wondered how strong it was in the country. The old Church of England was a bit ambiguous and you could treat church attendance as optional, whereas Catholics were obliged to attend. Quite a strong club to join! thought Robert.

Saturday dawned and after breakfast, Charles and Robert had decided to go to the local grass tennis courts to 'blow out the cobwebs'. Robert knew that Charles played for the local Reigate tennis club and that he had won the occasional tournament. Robert was not in that league but after work he had thrashed around on the hard courts on the local recreation ground near his parents home. He had met up with a couple of blokes from work for this activity and reached a competent self-taught standard. He made every effort to scrape the ball up and return it as it flew out of the court, and so was quite fast. His smoking did not help though and after he had recovered from the 'steel band round the chest' moment, he played on with quite a degree of fitness. He was not used to playing on grass courts and wondered how he would perform on these Reigate ones.

They started in a friendly manner, warming up and Charles, ever the competitive one, wanted match play. They played on for a couple of hours and amazingly Robert managed to hold his own against Charles. He found the grass courts were much slower than expected and he managed to get most of his returns back. He put this down largely to practising on hard courts, which he considered much faster with the ball spinning off rapidly. If you could return these you could return most. After two hours they declared it a draw and Charles said, 'I did not realise that you were such a good player as that, Bob.'

Robert replied, 'Well I have been getting some practice in of late,' and left it at that.

Robert felt happy that he had at least held his own against a Reigate tournament winner! He thought how he had never asked Juliet if she played tennis – in his next letter he would describe to her 'the famous Reigate tennis match'!

They retired to a nearby pub in town for a couple of pints to slake their thirst after the efforts of their play, and continued in jovial chat, remembering the funny points and incidents of their college days. That afternoon, they returned to the house for a bit of a sleep and a read after their exertions. In the evening there was a Young Conservatives gathering in the town hall with a guest speaker and wine and cheese afterwards. Charles was a sort of loose member and Robert was his guest. Robert had been Conservative by upbringing but was now apolitical. He found it rather odd how people could support a particular party with such conviction, but he supposed in time that might change even for him. The speaker was quite interesting, talking on local government, but the best part of the evening was the wine and cheesy things on sticks afterwards. Robert, as usual, drank too many glasses and was squiffy and engaged some attractive young women in conversation. They were rather interesting but shallow minded and he could not but help compare their natures with the sensible compassion of his Juliet.

Sunday arrived, and the other three Prestons had gone to an early mass. Robert and Charles slept on after their late wine drinking session the night before. Robert had been given a spare room at the back of the house and had been intrigued to see the replica statue of Rodin's 'Kiss' on the landing outside. The two lovers, naked, were intertwined in the most sensual manner as they executed their kiss. He could not help but be reminded of Juliet and his desire for her grew observing this statue, reminding him of their one, brief but sensual kiss. However, he was a little surprised that the Prestons had such a statue on display, knowing full well that he would never have seen such a one in his parental home!

Charles and Robert breakfasted late and the Sunday routine was to adjourn to the King's Head, that delightful little thatched pub just outside Reigate and down a lane, to spend the whole of Sunday lunchtime there drinking through to afternoon closing time, and then to return home for a late Sunday lunch. They arrived at the pub and it was full of many of Charles's friends and acquaintances, some of whom were at the Young Conservatives meeting the night before.

Pat and Neal were there as well, and Robert renewed his acquaintance with Neal. He was not a bad chap really but sometimes lacking common sense. He was an accountant of sorts but did not really fit into the same mindset as Robert and Charles. The afternoon wore on and Robert had become the centre of attraction to some admiring females when he told them of his adventure down on the rocket ranges. A little more rugged than the local solicitors and accountants that they were most used to. Yet he could not help but compare them to Juliet, and he found them so shallow in comparison.

The pub afternoon over, Charles and Robert returned to the house a little the worse for wear at about five o'clock. Charles's mother had the roast dinner waiting and as they ate, she enquired as to whom they had met that afternoon. Charles's father had spent the afternoon gardening and was ready for his meal. He asked of Charles, 'Did you get to mass, Charles?'

'No Father, but I'll be going tonight at seven.'

The meal was completed and it was Robert's cue to get ready for his return journey to London. He went and packed his grip and placed it in the hall next to the front door. He made his thank yous and farewells and was exhorted to return before too long, then went down the front steps to his waiting car accompanied by Charles. He said, 'Thanks again, Charles, we'll meet up again before too long and hopefully with George. Cheerio for now.' He drove off back in the direction of London as Charles stood waving him off in the road.

Chapter Sixteen

Robert felt very refreshed after his weekend down with Charles, and back in the parental London home again he was sitting contentedly with his parents that Sunday evening. The thought of work again tomorrow did not now seem so daunting after that weekend of refreshment and he felt ready for the undoubted challenges ahead that this career path had for him.

Monday morning came and Robert was up, washed and dressed with a new spring in his step. He breakfasted and was heading towards the front door when the sound of post falling through the letterbox reached his ears. He paused to pick up the letters and glanced through them. To his joy, there was one from Juliet. He thought that he would save reading it until the evening and put it on the hall table with the others. He left the house and walked to his car. It was one of the few cars in the road, and he left it parked on the road as the driveway between his parents' house and next door was too narrow to park in easily. The car started easily and he was soon out onto the Hendon bypass on the way to Stanmore.

The arrival in the office was jovial – Frank and Ben were there before him, puffing away on their pipes and discussing their respective weekends. Ben's sailing had gone rather well down at Hayling Island in Hampshire and Frank had rather a big Radio Ham sweep round the world – from his home base in London. Robert's entrance prompted their enquiries as to how his weekend had gone, and he related to them how he had fared in Reigate. With the mutual weekend exchange over and the arrival of the other engineers, they dispersed to brew up tea or coffee and to re-engage with the workloads on their desks and on their lab benches.

The morning seemed long after the weekend break and Robert was thankful when the lunch hour arrived so he could escape the rigorous schedule for a bit. The afternoon went better.

He had settled into the work routine by now and things were going more smoothly. He was close to completing his technical report on the feasibility of the upgraded guidance unit using the transistorised circuits. The circuit engineers, under his direction, had worked wonders in devising the new circuits and they had been thoroughly tested and were all working well. Robert's particular speciality of the guidance system had been tested on the antenna range and was working well but for a minor anomaly that needed ironing out. All this information had been compiled in the technical report and the first part of it was almost ready to be sent to the Ministry for their approval so that further project funding could be released.

The engineers left at 5 p.m. and Robert worked on until five thirty. Not his usual late hours today, but being Monday and after the busy weekend, it really was time for him to go!

He arrived home just after six and collected Juliet's letter from the hall table as he walked through the front door, breathing in with relish the smell of his mother's cooking.

'Is it you Robert? Hello my dear. Did you have a nice day? Mother will have the meal on the table soon, so go straight in and sit down. Your father will be back later tonight, he is attending a meeting at the bowls club.' Robert knew that his father had joined the office bowls club and that occasionally he had to attend extraordinary meetings after office hours. His father enjoyed it and it was his main activity outside of the normal family domestic scene. His mother and father would go to the occasional office do and to variety theatre shows, musicals and often to the cinema. Robert, when younger, had been taken to many of these shows and the cinema and was quite well versed in this sort of enter-tainment background. He had been impressed by a lot of what he had seen and it had moulded somewhat his tastes in humour and popular music.

His mother placed the plate of rabbit stew before him and sat down with hers. Robert put Juliet's letter to one side on the table and thought that good news was worth waiting for and that he would relish reading it later. His mother had become aware of Robert's connection with Juliet, whom she had met as Anne when visiting Tall Chimneys Farm with Hilda some years ago.

His mother was pleased with this connection as she liked Leon and Alice very much, and Anne and her brothers were thus of a very good family.

Robert ate. 'The stew's delicious, Mother,' he said.

'I'm pleased that you like it my dear, I'm sure your father will too. It's one of his favourites,' she responded.

A pudding of baked apples and custard followed. The apples were large stewing apples and with a liberal amount of demerara sugar were sufficiently sweetened so as to be memorable.

The table was cleared and cups of tea were taken into the lounge and supped seated in the comfort of the armchairs. His mother had her tea sugary as usual and Robert did not! The front door opened and closed and Robert's father walked in. 'Phew, that was some busy meeting. People do make an extraordinary fuss about trivial things,' he said.

'I'll get you a cup of tea, Percy my dear, go and sit yourself down.'

His father sat down, his mother brought the tea and Mr Brett explained to them both about the proceedings of his meeting at the bowls club. 'Percy my dear, your dinner is ready – come on through to the dining room,' said Robert's mother.

They went on through, leaving Robert alone in the lounge. It was an ideal opportunity for him to open the letter from Juliet and have a quiet read.

The letter began as usual. 'Dear Robert, I am so pleased that you have been getting on so well with your work, although you do seem to have to work so very hard and your time is so full with it all. I have thought often of you being down here with me and am always thinking of our short times together.' She went on, explaining the happenings on the farm, about her mother and father and brothers, and then the blow fell. 'I am currently in Truro hospital. I have been diagnosed with TB and am under observation in an isolation ward. You know when I met you on the train and I told you I had been staying with relatives in London? Well, I had in fact been visiting a specialist in Harley Street to try to find out what was wrong with me. It took a while for the diagnosis to be fully confirmed but it has come through now and I have to be in this special ward. You may remember when we were at your auntie's for Sunday lunch that I was a bit off-colour then... Well, I was because I knew the diagnosis had been confirmed then and I was not feeling too happy about it. They say that I probably contracted it working in the damp stables out on the farm. Mother and Father and the boys are devastated. I am coughing quite a bit at the moment and am infectious, so I cannot have any direct visitors, and that makes it all the harder. I have every chance of recovery as they have some modern drugs now to treat it, but it is very distressing. Please keep writing and sending me your news, as it is so interesting and cheers me up. Don't rush to come down or anything as you would not be allowed to see me, and it's better that I am left to recover fully.'

Robert gawped in amazement – he could not believe what he had been reading. 'Juliet with TB! I can't believe it, I can't believe it,' he muttered to himself. Would she recover? What would it do to her? What would it do to them? Would she pull through, and if so, what state of health would she be left in? These thoughts and others raced through his mind, and he felt as though he had been poleaxed by the news. How he could return to work tomorrow and carry on as normal? It was beyond thinking about! He sat there in the chair clutching the letter in his hand and could do very little else other than stay in that trance-like state that the news had sent him into.

His mother and father entered the room carrying cups of tea and his mother noticed immediately the change in Robert's demeanour. 'My dear, you look as though you have just seen a ghost!'

Robert was loath to say how prophetic indeed this possibility could be, but recovered sufficiently to blurt out, 'Yes, Mother, I have just heard that Juliet's ill. Please read the letter.'

His mother read in silence and then the letter was passed on to his father. His father read it and said, 'Well, there is every chance of her recovery, boy, with modern medicine and care. It's not so bad as the old days when most did not recover.' Percy realised that with this last utterance he might have gone too far so he shut up immediately.

Robert's parents were both very sympathetic and assured him that there was every possibility of an excellent recovery for Juliet.

Robert collected himself and immediately set himself to writing to Juliet and to her parents as well, and also a line to Aunt Hilda as she must have heard the bad news too.

Robert could not sleep very well that night. Thoughts of Juliet in that condition kept flying through his head. It was almost unbearable. I must get some sleep though, he thought, as I have to perform at work tomorrow. He went downstairs, found the drinks cabinet and poured himself a very stiff whisky, added water and sent it down the hatch. It had the desired effect of making him sleep, but he slept on later than usual and it was a mad rush for him to get to work on time. Unusually, he lit up a cigarette as soon as he left the house, to steady his nerves. Generally he did not light up until he got to work. The drive to work was a blur and he did not remember getting there. He entered the office and the others were already at their respective stations. Ben noticed his late arrival and made a jocular remark. 'One over the eight last night then, Bob?'

Robert could hardly respond. 'No Ben, but sorry I'm late – it won't happen again. I'm feeling slightly under the weather.'

Ben left him alone to settle in to the day and later said, 'We'll discuss that technical report of yours before it's sent off to the Ministry. It reads very well but needs a bit of editing, so in my office about eleven o'clock, OK?'

Robert said, 'OK Ben,' and then he slumped at his desk, hardly able to get organised.

The meeting went well and with some editing the report was in good enough condition to be forwarded to the Ministry. Their eventual response was: 'This is an excellent report and we concur with its findings and so you are authorised to proceed with the guidance unit upgrade.' This heartened Robert but did not compensate him for the pain and foreboding he felt about Juliet's condition.

The work continued with further trials at the Aberporth firing range and at the Pendine rocket ranges, and with plenty of laboratory updating of electronic units. Letters were sent between Robert and Juliet but it seemed that her replies were continually speaking of a deteriorating condition, much to the despair of Robert. Some months passed and her letters became less frequent.

Robert was beside himself with worry. He immersed himself in his work as much as he could, but thoughts of Juliet were never far away. Finally, the letters seemed to stop altogether. His last letter to her, three weeks previously, had not been replied to and Robert was so concerned that he wrote to Leon and Alice.

The reply came a week later. 'I am very sorry my boy, but Juliet passed away two weeks ago and we have just had her funeral in St Petroc's. I am very sorry that we did not tell you sooner and that the funeral has already taken place, but because of the infection we had to decide quickly on her burial. It was probably best that you did not come as it would have been so upsetting for you. Alice and I are both devastated and the boys too in losing their sister. I know you and her were getting along well and were very fond of each other but it was not to be. Please do not think too hard on us for not telling you earlier, but it's been a terrible time for us and we did not know whether we were coming or going most of the time. Your aunt is very upset too. We are all getting older now, and the loss of Juliet in has aged us considerably. Your aunt is more housebound now and could not get out herself to the funeral.' The letter went on with some more, less important news.

Robert was shattered by this news and was also very angry that he had not been informed of the funeral. Beside himself with grief, he immediately wrote a letter to Leon and to Alice and to his Aunt Hilda. What could he really say? He had just lost the love and hope of his life. He had envisaged their future with perhaps them settling down on the moor somewhere together. He would eventually have got a job down there. Now, it had all gone! Did he really have to forgo all that for a hard-working life in London, with the distinct possibility of no joy for the future? The pain in his head was considerable. It would be a waste of time going to Cornwall now to see any of them. He could not face them. Certainly not now! The magic had suddenly disappeared. His parents were devastated too and quite concerned for his state of health. He was smoking considerably more cigarettes now but did not care any more, and viewed life now through a constant blur of pain. Alone in his bed at night there was little relief, and with considerable shots of whisky he wept himself to sleep most nights.

Chapter Seventeen

Since the death of Juliet, Robert had plunged himself even more deeply into his work. He had been at AEI for a good five years now and the Sea Streak project was up to the mark IV version, and just prior to the Naval Acceptance Trials. Robert was a Principal Engineer by now and he and his team had ironed out the guidance principle by the introduction of a new, clever antenna system, and the guidance unit itself was now fully transistorised thanks to the efforts of his electronic engineers. The power and weight saving with this introduction was considerable, and this had a major effect on the increase of the missile's range and speed. Further sea trials were coming up soon, using the trials ship TS *Girdleness*, based in Portsmouth, and he would have to be present at some time during these trials.

By now he had moved out of the house since his father's retirement and his mother's death. This had saddened him immensely but he was now independent in his bachelor's flat closer to Stanmore. It wasn't bad, catering for all his needs with two bedrooms, although every time he entered the door he was always struck by the silence and lack of other human company. He called in on his father as often as he could on the way home from work and was surprised at how well the old man was coping on his own. He could muster his own meals, do light housework and went off to the bowls club at weekends. He was managing well on his pension, which was a good company one after forty-five years of service.

One of the regrets that Robert had with respect to the passing of his mother was that his father had decided to have her cremated at Golders Green crematorium, and Robert would have preferred a burial as it would have allowed him to visit a grave rather than an area of land where her ashes had been scattered. Though since the death of Juliet and her hasty burial, Robert had not even enquired as to where she was buried, but he suspected that it was in Bodmin cemetery. He still had not visited Cornwall since that fateful day of hearing of her death, but he had been in a better frame of mind lately over the matter and was contemplating a visit in the not too distant future, if his frantic working schedule would allow. As a Principal Engineer, his salary had increased considerably and he did not have to worry about money any more. Ben was still project leader and Frank was still over him but it had been intimated as he had done so well on Sea Streak that he would be first in line for the next proposed missile project, Sea Wing, a defence weapon with a shorter range, to protect individual ships from any attacking aircraft breaking through the area defence coverage of Sea Streak. He had already been looking at the naval requirements for this missile, and had formulated some *a priori* ideas.

He had met up with Charles a few times over the last couple of years and had gone with him to the wedding of George and Delia, who had settled in Staines, so socially he had his outlets with his good friends. But the hollowness of the loss of Juliet was still with him inside. He had met one or two girls in the meantime and had taken them out to various venues, but in no time at all his uncompromising discernment crept in and he lost interest in them. Too scatty or too stupid or lacking those indefinable characteristics that had made Juliet his ideal girl. Would he ever meet anybody at all? Well, that was in the lap of the gods, or in God's lap, depending on your point of view!

Work continued at its usual pace and everything was arranging itself towards the sea trials. Robert had liaised with the trial team, currently based in Portsmouth near the ship but governed from Stanmore. The trial testing and tuning documentation was produced by his department and the trials team had to be perfectly au fait with the procedures, so this necessitated trial team instruction sessions that took place at Stanmore, but the final preparation procedures would have to be gone over on the ship in Portsmouth.

Robert was sitting at home in his flat one evening when the telephone rang. He finally had it installed for the convenience of not having to walk to the box on the corner on dark, wet, winter nights. Mind you, the off-licence was nearby and it was always convenient to pop in and replenish his Scotch and the Bordeaux red that he had an increasing penchant for.

He lifted the handset, half expecting Charles, but it was Simeon his cousin.

'Is that Rob?' said the voice. 'It's Simeon here, how are you getting on?'

This was an unprecedented call from his cousin. They exchanged Christmas cards and notes a couple of times a year, but very rarely a phone call.

'Simeon, it's good to hear from you. How are you, and how is John and all at Porth?'

'They are all OK, thank you, Rob. Aggie and Mum and Dad are all getting older and not so mobile as they used to be, but Aunt Hilda has had a stroke at home and she is now in the cottage hospital in Bodmin. They don't give her too long to live.'

Robert was stunned to think that Aunt Hilda, that invincible Bodmin institution, had succumbed thus. He had considered her immortal and not subject to such things as this. They talked on for some time, with Robert finally asking Simeon to keep him informed of developments.

Barely a fortnight had elapsed when the inevitable phone call came informing him of the death of his aunt. Robert, though expecting this, was nevertheless deeply saddened by her passing, thinking that Bodmin would never be the same again. He said that he would very much want to attend the funeral of his favourite aunt, and would Simeon please tell him of the times and arrangements well beforehand, remembering the debacle over Juliet's arrangements. Simeon said he would without fail, and Robert left the matter in his cousin's hands.

Robert continued with his work, anticipating the call from Simeon any time. Soon enough, the call came. The funeral had been arranged for a Friday, and so he would have to travel down on the Thursday. To cover this, he would have to book a couple of days' leave from work. It was convenient that the weekend followed directly and this would give him some leisure time before he needed to return. In spite of the circumstances, he was looking forward to a return trip to Cornwall and to Bodmin. It would blow away the cobwebs of the old ghosts. He would see his relatives again, and he might even visit Juliet's grave as well. He wondered how Leon and Alice were getting along now.

The next day was Tuesday, and he had the opportunity to ask Ben for the time off for the funeral. Ben said that he could have the time off but he would have to go into Portsmouth on the way down to help the trials team complete the preparations for the sea trial. So he would have to travel down on Sunday night, book in somewhere to stay, and spend Monday to Wednesday with the trials team. Then and only when the trials preparation arrangements were complete could he go on his way to Cornwall on the Thursday.

Robert breathed a sigh. 'Thanks, Ben,' he said. It was all working out to schedule as he had hoped! Robert lit up a cigarette, coughed profusely and walked off back to his desk to make the appropriate arrangements. He asked their secretary to book him into Kepples Head Hotel next to the dockyard gate. This was where the visiting engineers normally stayed, as it was so close to the dockyard and convenient for walking in. He then proceeded to book himself into a bed and breakfast in Bodmin for Thursday and Friday and provisionally Saturday as well. The place was just at the top end of Castle Hill, close to the moor. He had seen it advertised, rung the proprietor and been told that they had vacancies as it was late August and getting on towards September. Strange, he thought, that he would be returning to Bodmin about the same time of the year as when he had last stayed there over five years ago! This time, of course, he had his car and would not be travelling down there on the train.

On the way home from work he called in to see his father and told him of the arrangements. His father said, 'Give my best to Aggie and all and tell them that I am sorry I can't get there myself. Take care, Rob, on your journey.' His father closed the door behind him as Robert headed on back to his flat.

Sunday afternoon soon came round and Robert was on his way to Portsmouth down through Guilford, Esher, Hindhead and Petersfield. The journey was very pleasant in the afternoon sun, although he noticed already the shadow of autumn falling as he saw the browning leaves on some of the trees. After about two hours he was driving up Portsdown hill, past The George, a pub on the left and over the brow of the hill to briefly view that panoramic view of the very built-up Portsea Island with the Solent and the hills of the Isle of Wight beyond. The Solent forts, part of 'Palmerston's Follies', stood out crystal clear in the water. What a view!

He drove down into the environs of the city over Portsea Island Bridge and was soon in the traffic snarl-ups further down in town. He saw the signs to Southsea and the sea front and kept driving straight on as he had been advised. 'Drive on to the seafront and turn right to The Hard – you can't miss it!' He did that and after some stopping and starting eventually saw the sign for Kepples Head Hotel and drove into the small car park alongside. He booked in at the reception desk and was briefly shown the large bar and the magnificently furnished dining room before being escorted upstairs to a single bedroom on the first floor and overlooking The Hard. From The Hard the ferries to Gosport and to the Isle of Wight plied their seemingly never-ceasing trade. He sat in the window seat for a while, smoking a cigarette and observing the scene, much quieter on a Sunday no doubt, before turning to unpack his grip bag and placing his briefcase with his technical papers in the wardrobe along with his spare clothes and funeral suit.

He awoke early on Monday morning and rose for breakfast. Breakfast was from seven to nine thirty, catering for naval officers to join their ships early and for visiting contractors. After breakfast he returned to his room, dressed appropriately for the day 'afloat' and gathered the papers in his briefcase. A dockyard policeman directed him in the direction of the *Girdleness* after he had signed the appropriate contractors' paperwork. She was moored against the north west wall of the dockyard, looking out towards Whale Island and Porchester Castle, ready to leave for trials. Robert walked up past the *Victory* and reminded himself that he should visit her one day and walked past numerous sheds and docks, some with ships being refitted and some without, until he reached the *Girdleness*. She was rather ugly, grey and built purely for utility, but served her purpose well as a trials ship. The Sea Streak launcher was well forward and the radar-tracking tower was well aft. He went up the gangway and made his way to the bridge control room, avoiding tripping over endless cables that snaked over the deck and into various compartments. He met up again with the trials team, and they started going over the endless procedures, making amendments and notes as they discovered discrepancies and anomalies.

He was glad when the first day of this was over and he could return to the hotel. The next two days passed in a similar style of intense activity, and various firing and tracking procedures were simulated on the racks of built-in guidance transponder equipment. Robert was very pleased when Wednesday evening arrived and all the test procedure checks had been carried out successfully. That evening in the hotel restaurant he treated himself to a Steak Dianne with a good bottle of Bordeaux, followed by crepe Suzettes and Viennese coffee. Tomorrow was his trip to Cornwall and it would be a long day. As he lay in bed that night, he reflected again on the loss of Juliet and only wished that this time he was going to meet her.

Chapter Eighteen

Robert left the Kepples Head Hotel early on Thursday morning. He wanted to leave promptly so he would not arrive too late in Bodmin. As he was going from Portsmouth and not from London, he would follow mainly the south coast route and not down the middle of the country as he would have done from London. He drove out of Portsmouth on the western side of the city and turned off on to the A27 on the way to Porchester and on the road to Southampton. Going through the centre of Southampton, he drove through the New Forest, past Ringwood and took the road to Wimborne and on to Bere Regis past one of the longest estate walls he had ever seen, and arrived at Dorchester just before midday.

He parked up in the high street outside the Judge Jeffery's Restaurant and decided to have an early lunch there. It broke his journey and was approximately the halfway point. He walked into the restaurant and found it quite deserted. He sat down at a table for two by the window overlooking the high street. An attractive young waitress came up to him, dressed in a red and white checked frock with a white apron. She asked him what he would like, and he chose the standard set lunch for the day. Roast beef, roast potatoes and two veg, to be followed by apple pie and custard or a choice of ice cream or biscuits and cheese.

As he sat eating, he read the historic write-up on the wall next to his table about Judge Jeffery's 'Bloody Assizes' that were held there in the 1660s. Apparently the judge had decided to hang most of those who had participated in any respect in the rebellion, whatever their pleas of mitigation under the circumstances. This was terrible, thought Robert. How could he pre-judge the situation of each person without taking individual circumstances into account? This certainly would not happen today under British justice, he thought.

He finished his lunch. It was very good. The waitress came to the table to ask whether he wanted anything else. He said, 'Just the bill, please,' and feeling well disposed, had a short chat with her. She had a very pleasant, warm manner. So different from the town girls he so often came across. If he could have stayed in this area, he might even have ventured to ask her out.

He returned to his car and was soon at the western end of Dorchester, driving past the radio station on the right and on his way towards Bridport. He was smoking and flicking the cigarette ash out of the partially open drivers window. Irritatingly, some of it did blow back in if you were not careful. He wondered if it might have been easier on the train – less concentration and more leisurely – but it seemed by now that he had become very much dependent on his car. The weather was fine with good visibility, but as he progressed west he noticed darker clouds in the sky and hoped that it would not rain, as the car windscreen wipers were most inefficient. They were driven from a vacuum chamber that changed in pressure according to the engine revolutions, having a most variable effect on the wiper speed, from dead slow to moderate. This was not good in driving rain conditions!

He had a clear run through Bridport and then on to Honiton and Exeter. From Exeter, he drove across the magnificent rugged scenery of Dartmoor and through Okehampton. Just before reaching Launceston, he crossed the River Tamar and really felt then that he was in Cornwall. There was an old saying that the devil had not been allowed to cross over into Cornwall from the mainland, and that once in Cornwall all your worries were left behind. This effect did indeed seem to happen as he experienced a sense of relief and well being now in the land of 'Kernow'!

He decided to have a brief stop in Launceston before journeying on the last twenty miles or so to Bodmin. He parked the car in a side street and walked in to the town centre. A very pretty little market town it was, and he strolled around taking in the shops and smoking a cigarette. He noticed the monument commemorating and indicating the spot where Cuthbert Mayne, the Catholic martyr, had been executed for his faith in 1577. Beyond, just outside of the town was Launceston Castle, where Mayne had been imprisoned for a long time under adverse conditions. Ironically so too had George Fox, the founder of the Quakers, a century later in the same dungeon, but then to a different form of faith that certainly would not have been sympathetic to Catholicism. Surprisingly, his aunt, who was high Church of England, had pointed out the Cuthbert Mayne memorial to him years ago. She must have had some sympathy for the martyr, although she was certainly for the national church without the nonsense of Roman interference, as she would have put it!

He resumed his journey on the last twenty miles to Bodmin, crossing over now the bleak, mysterious, magnificent scenery of Bodmin moor. As he drove past Jamaica Inn he was seized with a deep nostalgia as he remembered his meeting with Juliet there five years ago, and their return motorbike journey to the farm with her hanging on so tightly to him on the pillion seat. He drove past and was soon at the sign to Temple and the turning opposite towards St Breward direction was the turning he had taken to Mentreaths Farm, Tall Chimneys to meet Juliet with his aunt and then a later time on the motorbike. He felt very much drawn to go there but dared not. It would never be the same again! He drove on past Cardingham Down and Racecourse Farm viewing the beacon in the westerly direction, which loomed more significantly over the town the closer he approached. He entered the top end of the town and down into Castle Hill, past the camp site, and he spied the bed and breakfast sign up on the left and braked the car to a halt alongside the house. It was called Bodmin Heights, a most appropriate name for its position, and he was pleased that he had found it so conveniently.

He took his grip out of the boot and walked up the pathway to the house and rang the doorbell. A plumpish lady answered and said with a most significant Cornish accent, 'Is it Mr Brett then?'

His identity was confirmed and he was invited in. She was most hospitable and he was shown his very comfortable bedroom and then invited into the homely lounge for a cup of tea and a saffron bun. She was rather interrogative as to why he was down here staying toward the end of the season, and he did volunteer the information that he was down for his aunt's funeral tomorrow. 'Mrs Yudy, did you know her?' he said.

'Bless my soul, I most certainly did. I used to talk to her often in town at Mr Bray's, and I'm so sorry for your loss, but she did have a good innings.'

This was straight Cornish talk, stating the facts! Robert however was not offended and said, 'Yes, she certainly lived a good long life and certainly had her innings.'

'She was so well respected in the town and we won't see her like again in a hurry.' responded the Landlady.

Robert drank his tea and ate his bun and made a move to go to his room. She said, 'Would you like an evening meal? I can certainly do one for you if you like.'

It was 6 p.m. by now, as indicated by the faint, distant chimes of St Petroc's church bell. 'No thank you. I had a cooked lunch and I am not too hungry at the moment,' he said. 'I'll just settle in, unpack and rest up for the funeral day tomorrow. It's not until 11 a.m. so I'll have plenty of time to walk down there,' he said.

'You're most welcome to come down to the lounge later to spend the evening there. You're the only guest I have at the moment, so it will be nice and quiet in there for you,' she said.

Robert unpacked his things and hung up his funeral suit to allow any creases to fall out. He spent some time in the lounge reading the Cornish *Guardian* and then retired to bed around 10 p.m.

The following morning, he was faced with an enormous Cornish hogs pudding breakfast. He was pleased, as he was feeling peckish, after not having had an evening meal previously. It would set him up for the ordeal of the day ahead.

The morning passed slowly but eventually it was time for him to dress up in his funeral suit and make his way down to the church. The butterflies were fluttering in his tummy and he endeavoured to keep his general nervousness under control. The landlady said that he was looking extremely smart in his dark-blue suit with a hint of an undeclared stripe in it. He had purchased it at Perry Grant's, the tailor, St. John's Road, Clapham Junction, on one of his London outings and it had stood him in good stead for a few years. It was bespoke made with hand-stitched collar and the trouser bottoms broke just on the insteps of his highly-polished black shoes.

He walked out of the B&B and turned left down Castle Hill towards the church. It was a fairly easy downhill walk and he heard the church bell chiming the quarter to the hour. Plenty of time to arrive punctually he thought. He had reached his aunt's house now and looked in through the kitchen window as he passed. How forlorn it all seemed, and how old. He looked across at Miss Mudge's opposite and that looked deserted too, as though no one was living there any more. He heard no livestock sounds and did not notice any chickens strutting around. Has Miss Mudge passed on also? he thought to himself. He drew in deeply on his cigarette and glanced in at his aunt's garden as he passed. It was beginning to get unkempt and looking back towards the front door showed him such a deserted look. Across the road at Mrs Sandow's there was a similar impression of quiet desertion and he wondered what had been happening to the old place during his absence of five years.

He walked on down to the steps to St Petroc's and found that at least one thing was still going – the gurgling spring water issuing from the granite wall. He let the water flow over his hands and applied some to his face to freshen himself up. The late summer sun was shining well and it would be a good day.

He walked into the church and the tableau that greeted him was of his aunt's coffin lying before the altar, with a substantial congregation assembled and seated either side. He was not late and was surprised to see them assembled so early. The organ was playing low, suitably-pitched music for the solemnity of the occasion. He felt quite choked up seeing his aunt's coffin lying there and almost started shaking with emotion. He checked himself and was saved from wondering where to sit by a sidesman asking him whether he was family or a friend. Robert said 'family', and was conducted to the three front rows of seats on the left-hand side of the church. Thankfully he noticed his two cousins, Simeon and John there, and slid in beside them in a spare seat. They greeted one another as best they could in hushed tones, and Robert enquired as to their parents and Aggie. He was told that due to their advancing years, none of them were up to making the journey to the funeral. He did wonder who most of these people were – generally friends, he thought, recognising one or two faces from the past.

The organ struck up the hymn, 'For all the saints who from their labours rest...' The vicar and his entourage processed in, attired suitably for a funeral. The service began, 'My brothers and sisters, we are gathered here today in the sight of Almighty God to perform these funeral rites for our recently, dearly departed sister, Hilda Yudy, late of this parish...' The service continued with further prayers and hymns, and was very moving. The final committal came prior to the processing out and Robert had to resort to his handkerchief, as did many others, he had noticed. The final processional hymn came. 'Love divine all loves excelling, joy of heaven to earth came down...' A most appropriate hymn and undoubtedly it would have been his aunt's favourite. The pallbearers moved out to pick up the coffin and Robert was surprised to see James, Giles and John Mentreath acting as pallbearers with another chap he did not recognise. Juliet's brothers! He did not know whether he had expected to see them here and if so, certainly not performing this role. The coffin entourage processed down the aisle, making its way towards the church door. It was all a bit of an emotional blur for Robert, and as one of the principal mourners he followed the coffin out in the first group of people, not noticing who was still seated or who was following.

He was nearing the door and then the blow came. An arm tugged him out of the procession and a female voice said, 'Robert, Robert, is it you?'

He turned to confront the person and what befell his gaze was the most astounding view he had encountered for years. It was Juliet! He was staggered – he was stunned – he could hardly believe his eyes. 'Juliet, I thought you were dead,' he groaned.

She pulled him further away from the funeral procession to a quieter part of the church. 'Well, I am not,' she responded and went on, 'Oh Robert, I am so sorry. It was so unfair of them to tell you I had died, it must have been awful for you and totally unforgivable of my parents.'

Robert had tuned ashen and had to sit down in a pew. Juliet sat with him. 'I was so ill with TB at the time and nobody thought that I would live. I did pull through, though but it took me months to recover and I did not repair to full health anyway – I am a bit of an invalid now. They thought it would be kinder to tell you that I had died, so that you would not be saddled with an invalid, as you had all of your life and career before you. I was too ill anyway at the time to do anything about it, and was really unaware as to what their plans were. When I was strong enough and found out, it was too late. I sort of went along with it thinking that I would always be an invalid and in too poor health for you anyway. I did love you though, Robert, always.' Robert still looked at her as though he had seen a ghost. He did not know what to say. He felt choked by what he had heard and by the deception practised. He looked closely into Juliet's face. Yes, she did look older, and more pinched and frail. Her previously robust figure also looked fragile and thin. She smiled at him. It was the same disarming smile that he remembered, in spite of her frail looks. 'You must think awfully of me,' she said, 'and particularly on meeting up on this occasion of your auntie's funeral. I thought you might have given up on Cornwall and would never come again.'

Still stunned and shocked, he did warm to her a little, almost prepared to forgive the past. 'Can I have a proper talk with you before I go back to London? We had better move on in the procession now, though, as they are moving off and we will be late for the burial.'

'Yes,' she said, and the next blow came, 'but I am married now.'

Robert took the blow but hardly realised what she had said. 'Where do you live now, then?' he said.

'It's further down the lane from Tall Chimneys. It's a bungalow called Sunny Bank and it's the only one on past the farmhouse, you can't miss it.'

'If we don't get time to talk today after the funeral, can I please call in and see you tomorrow on my way back to London?' he said.

'Yes, Robert,' she said. 'I'll look forward to that, come when you are ready. I don't stray too far from there these days.'

They rejoined the funeral procession and followed it round on foot to Bodmin cemetery. They did not speak on the way. There were no more interments in the churchyard, as it was full. The last rites were performed at the graveside. Robert and Juliet cast the earth down on to the aunt's coffin. The various groups split up and went their separate ways. Juliet returned to the moor with her brothers, saying to Robert that she would see him tomorrow, and Robert retired to the Hole in the Wall pub with his cousins and some others from the party and had an a la carte funeral breakfast, with plenty of liquid refreshment. His cousins thought that he was looking remarkably well. They did not know about his recent encounter with one whom he had just discovered had returned from the dead!

Back at the B&B, he informed the landlady of his intention to move on tomorrow and told her about the proceedings of the funeral – but did not, of course, mention the meeting with Juliet.

He left the next day, Saturday, after a hearty breakfast and was seen off by the landlady with a packet of sandwiches for his lunch. He thanked her very much and drove off up Castle Hill, across the moor past Cardingham Down on the way to Temple and turned left in the direction of St Breward and managed to find his way to Mentreaths Farm. Passing that farmhouse that was so significant to him, he wondered about Leon and Alice and how they were getting on. He would ask Juliet when he met her. He drove on down the lane and soon came across the bungalow. 'Sunny Bank' was emblazoned on a large slate slab at the entrance in gold letters. He turned into the drive and stopped the car. He saw Juliet pottering about in the rear section of the garden. She had heard the car door slam shut, and walked over to him.

'Robert. How lovely you came.'

'I had to Juliet, you knew that I would come. I have to talk to you! How are your parents, by the way?'

'Oh Robert, that is another tragedy. Father was taken ill with his heart three years ago and subsequently died. Mother pined for him so much that she only outlasted him by about a year. The boys now run Tall Chimneys together, and are making a good job of it.'

'I'm sorry to hear about your parents, Juliet, my condolences, but now how about you?'

'Robert, come inside and we'll sit down and have a chat over a cup of tea or coffee.' They sat down in a modern-furnished lounge with a large panoramic window overlooking the garden. Rather different to Tall Chimneys Farm, he thought.

'After Mother's and Father's deaths and the reorganising of the farm commitments, I was at a loss what to do. I looked after the boys for a while but was not strong enough to work as previously. I used to go to Young Farmers and there was a friend of the boys there, Joseph Trebilcock. He proposed to me one day and as I was a bit lonely, I accepted. We now live here in this bungalow that father had bought some time ago and had rented out to farm workers. Joe was one of those and had been living here in the past.' Juliet saw how dismayed Robert looked on hearing this and said, 'Yes Robert, I should have contacted you and told you the truth about my illness, but time went by and it was so easy to do this. Joe is a good man and has always been part of the farming community around here.'

Robert perceived a slight here. Maybe unintentional, but nevertheless it seemed that she was telling Robert that a farmer's girl always preferred a farming man. He did sense however that the marriage had probably been arranged on lines of convenience and thought that she probably did not love her husband as she ought to.

She said, 'Oh Robert, I did not mean it in that way. I did love you very much and had hoped that we could have got together, but because of that dreadful TB it did not work out.'

Robert said, 'Do you mind if I smoke?'

'Go on, then,' she said, and they both laughed, sensing the disapproval in her voice. 'But outside, please.'

They walked out into the garden, he walking and smoking, she walking and deadheading flowers. Robert coughed. 'Oh, you should really give that up, it's not at all good for your chest and lungs.'

Robert brushed this rebuke off and said, 'Juliet, I really would have liked to marry you.'

'I know, Robert,' she said, 'me too, but it's too late now, sadly.'

Robert looked at her, wanting to take her into his arms but held back. He could not encroach on another man's marriage; it would not be correct! 'By the way,' he said, 'where is Joe?'

'He's down with the boys on the farm making hay in the top fields.'

Robert remembered that last time he was here, the same procedures were going on. 'Well Juliet, I must be getting on my way,' he said, realising a their full reunion would be impossible now. 'If you have any children, name one after me.'

'That won't be possible,' she said, 'the doctors said that I can't have any after my illness.'

Robert said, 'Goodbye, Juliet ' and leaned over and kissed her on the cheek, longing to touch her lips with his kiss, but resisting. He clasped both her hands and then broke away, walking to the car. He turned and said, 'Don't die on me again, I may want to visit you sometime.'

She smiled lovingly at him and he backed the car out of the drive and was gone off down the lane waving his arm from the window.

Well, that was that, he thought as he traced his path back to the main road. He lit up a cigarette and drove off across the moor. The craggy tors were fast disappearing either side of him and soon he was out of that magical land, Cornwall, into Devon on his way back to the great metropolitan city of London.

Chapter Nineteen

Robert arrived back in London around 5 p.m. It had been a long journey and most of the way back, he had been turning over in his mind the incredible events of the past couple of days. It was astounding. He could hardly believe that Juliet was really alive. He had not been conversing with a ghost, had he? No, she was real all right. One thing that this trip had done for him though was to purge his system of her. He knew what the situation was. She was married now and clearly beyond his reach, and strangely enough it gave him almost a sense of tranquillity and now that he did not have to mourn her loss any more. The possibility of an improved future actually dawned on him now – he could move on!

He arrived at his Stanmore flat, parked up and went indoors. Tomorrow was Sunday and so he could rest up prior to work. He thought he would go round to his father's tomorrow, to tell him the news of the trip and the funeral and perhaps take him out for Sunday lunch somewhere.

Robert arrived at his father's on Sunday and was cordially greeted by him. His father listened intently as Robert explained to him all the ins and outs of the trip and the funeral and the fact that Aggie, Gi and Jack had not attended. 'They must be getting old and past it, just like me,' he said.

Robert made no comment but sadly was beginning to realise that some of his relatives probably would not be with them much longer. He did not tell his father of the reappearance of Juliet, as that might have had a distressing effect on him. 'Come on then, Dad, let's go out for a Sunday lunch. Where would you recommend?'

His father said, 'The Coaching House on Hampstead Heath is a good place to go. They do a very good lunch there and they are licensed premises and there is a good outlook.'

'OK then, Dad, that's where we'll go.' They drove in the direction of Hampstead Heath, passing a single Decker 226 bus that they often used to take on their journeys up there in the past. The lunch was very pleasant, particularly enhanced by the outlook across the parkland towards the trees. They had lamb cutlets, pomme frites and a mixed tureen of vegetables, washed down with pints of bitter. They finished with strawberry tart and coffee. Afterwards they had a stroll around the heath, smoking their cigarettes and walked up to the pond where all the children were fishing with their parents in attendance near by. That evening, Robert returned his father home and then returned to his flat. As he walked in, he sensed immediately the all-pervading silence but chose to ignore it. He made himself a cup of coffee and sat with it in his favourite armchair, lit up a cigarette and reflected over recent events. It had been an extraordinary week, what with the work in Portsmouth, his aunt's funeral, the 'resurrection' of Juliet, but now, he thought, he would have to put his mind back on to the project at work – it was still very pressing. He would go back to AEI tomorrow to face the pressures again, so as soon as he finished his coffee, he retired early to get a good night's sleep.

Next morning, back at AEI, the pressure was immediately on. When he was away in Cornwall, three missiles were fired by the trials team on the *Girdleness* and only one out of the three was completely successful. One failed to obtain guidance at all and the other only obtained guidance intermittently. There was a stack of trials test reports on his desk and Ben was furiously puffing away at his pipe saying, 'We really have to solve this one, or heads are going to roll.'

Robert lit up a Players medium and inhaled deeply, but started coughing almost immediately. On recovering from this bout of coughing he said, 'Well Ben, I'm your man, guidance is my responsibility and if I can't solve it, nobody can!'

Ben took the hint and calmed down a bit. 'OK, Bob. We're now under enormous pressure and I am relying on you and your boys. Those results need analysing immediately, and the solution must be in hand before a fortnight otherwise the Ministry police will be down to take me away!'

Robert laughed at this hyperbole from Ben. He knew he was exaggerating, but nevertheless he was fully aware of the seriousness of the situation. 'I'm right on to it now, Ben, and I'll be bringing you the solution as soon as I have it.'

With that he crushed out his cigarette in the ashtray, lit up another, slung his jacket over the back of his chair and commenced pouring over the trials data. Ben walked away back to his own office, realising that it was better to leave him alone for the moment.

Three days passed and Robert was hard at it, and edging closer to a solution. With the help of his 'boys', it seemed that the transistorised guidance unit, as it was produced in a hurry, had been assembled without metal screening around the critical input amplifiers and it had been picking up stray RF signals that had become demodulated, and then were conducted to alter the control of the guidance vanes. The solution seemed to be a reconstruction of the unit so as to screen and separate the critical areas out from the non-critical. This seemed relatively simple but in fact was a major redesign layout and reconstruction that would take weeks.

All this pressure had been getting to him and he had taken to walking out in the lunch hours rather than staying fixed to his desk, mulling over the problems while eating sandwiches. He even avoided the canteen for a while, as too much shop was being discussed there over the dinner table. The late September weather was still good with the occasional rain shower or two, but in the main it was good. His walk out was in pleasant sunshine and he had taken to walking in the grounds of a church just off the high street. It was a modern building as far as churches went. Probably only fifty years old. Certainly not as old and venerable as St Petroc's, Bodmin! He had ventured to go in, and found it so quiet and peaceful that it relaxed him entirely and bolstered him for his afternoon's work back at the lab. He had taken to calling in at the church once or twice a week and noticed that a few other people were there regularly kneeling before the altar and saying prayers. The minister or priest would occasionally walk down the aisle and lean over and chat to a parishioner, and eventually noticed the regular appearances of Robert. So, one day, he leaned over to have a hushed chat with him.

'I noticed that you come in here quite often, but you're not a regular parishioner, are you?'

'No, I'm not,' replied Robert, 'but I pop in here occasionally. It's so peaceful and the relaxation helps me to carry on with my work.' He then explained briefly his background and the pressure of his work.'

'Well, I'm Father Ignatius and if I can be of any help to you, you only need to ask. The presbytery, that is, the priests' house, is at the bottom of the church garden and you can always call to have a chat. If I am not there, my housekeeper will always make an appointment for you.'

'Thank you, er… er… Father, I will certainly do that if I need your help. Thank you.'

With that, the priest walked away. Robert thought, yes this must be a Catholic church, what with him being called Father; I never really noticed that it was. When he left, he noticed a somewhat obscure notice board that said 'Sacred Heart Roman Catholic Church, Stanmore, Mass times…' I wonder why I never noticed that before, he thought to himself, and then walked on back to work.

Back at work, the pressure held up for a further few weeks. This continued until the revised guidance units came completed out of production. They were then ready for submitting for further trials on the Sea Streak missile. The testing and tuning programme for the revised units was going ahead, designed and supervised by Robert. They had to meet the trials programme ordained for late October and early November. The pressure was on again for Robert and one evening, feeling rather down at his flat on his own, he ventured to call Father Ignatius to arrange a meeting. Father Ignatius seemed to have an incredible understanding of human nature and was most sympathetic to Robert's plight of being under enormous pressure. He even intimated to him that he felt under such pressure when studying for the priesthood at the English college in Rome. Latin was not his strong subject, and he had to have hours of extra tuition before he became anywhere near competent in the subject. Without the Latin he would not have been allowed to be a priest.

There was no ulterior motive behind these meetings in respect of converting Robert to the Catholic faith, but the snippets that Robert was inevitably picking up on was making the subject grow attractive. Such peace and balm seemed to be emitted from Father Ignatius and from the other Catholics he had recently met. Father Ignatius understood that Robert had admired courageous people such as Scott of the Antarctic and Shackleton, and any great adventurer. Strangely enough, the majority of these people's courage and inspiration came from their faith, and Father Ignatius sensed this and asked Robert if he would like to borrow a copy of Butler's *Lives of the Saints*. 'I think that you will find a number of courageous characters in there to read about,' he said.

At their next meeting, Robert said that he was moved when reading some of their lives, particularly the Roman soldiers who in the early days of Christianity had refused to give up their faith and had been laid out to die in icy water – not one of them refuted the faith and they all froze to death. He was also moved by St Ignatius Loyola, that Spanish nobleman soldier, who, when recovering from a war injury, had converted to Christianity when reading of the lives of the saints, and then went on to demonstrate great courage himself in defence of the faith and became the founder of the Jesuits. 'I took my name from him' said Father Ignatius.

Robert continued with the missile programme, having successfully completed the trials programme. Three out of three missiles were guided perfectly, all thanks to Robert and his team's redesign of the guidance unit. Ben called Robert into his office.

'We and the Ministry are very pleased with the success of the Sea Streak project, and now want to appoint you as Project Leader of the short range Sea Wave missile development programme.'

Robert was very pleased to hear this news and accept the accolade, but feared the pressure of another intensive development programme.

He started the programme off a couple of weeks later and the familiar pressure points and heavy work schedule soon started up. He was smoking heavily again and his cough was getting worse. At a progress meeting, Ben and Frank both noticed this and Frank said, 'For heavens' sake, Bob, you've got a heck of a cough there. You really ought to go and see the Quack!'

Robert did not really want to go but realised he ought to and on the next visit to his father's, he got the address of his father's doctor, Dr Knight in Golders Green. Robert was granted an afternoon off work for the appointment he made. Dr Knight was every inch the gentleman, and he examined Robert's chest with the dignity of an old-time doctor. The diagnosis came.

'Mr Brett, you do have a restricted breathing problem, but I do not have the facilities here to examine you further. I will write you this note so you can see a chest specialist and have your chest x-rayed at the Royal Hendon Hospital.'

The following week, he attended the specialist and was subjected to a number of chest x-rays. 'Thank you, Mr Brett,' said the specialist, 'we'll let you know the outcome of the x-rays. Expect a letter within a fortnight.'

Robert was back at work in the meantime, continuing with the new development programme, and was glad at the approach of the weekend. He did not work that Saturday morning and was pleased of the break. He came downstairs in his dressing gown and was feeling quite chesty. He picked up the mail from the doormat and read the address on the brown, formal-looking envelope. It was from the Hendon Hospital, and he opened it with trembling hands. It read:

'Dear Mr Brett,

Further to your recent chest x-rays, I have to inform you that unfortunately we have discovered a spot on your lung and we would like you to attend as an in-patient on the twenty-fifth of November and stay in for further investigation of your condition...'

This came as a blow, and he sat down in the chair. He recovered sufficiently to make himself some coffee and drank it strong and black. He lit up a cigarette but the coughing fit it brought on made him stub it out almost immediately. Good Lord, he thought, that's next Thursday then. Must be a bit critical to want me in so quickly!

He dressed and went round to see his father, but couched it in terms of a routine check-up and told him not to worry. His father accepted the explanation and said, 'I hope it all goes well then, son.'

Robert left his house and busied himself with shopping for his weekend groceries and some to last him up to next Wednesday from Cricklewood Broadway.

Back at work on Monday, he had to go and tell Frank and Ben and get their permission for some time off from work. He would have to use mostly his annual leave entitlement for his hospital stay, but as a concession the company would give him some additional days of paid leave. He instructed his current Principal Engineer, Mike Broomfield, to cover the new development aspects in his absence, but did say that he could always be contacted at the hospital to give his advice on any problematic areas of the work.

Thursday came, and he had packed his grip bag and was off for an early morning entry into the hospital. He had dropped a note to Father Ignatius, telling him where he was going and that he would take his book in with to try and complete reading it. He was fortunate as he was placed in a private room in the hospital and not in a main ward. It gave him privacy and peace to think his own thoughts without having to communicate with others too much. Besides, did he not have to do that all day at work? And, at the moment, he was feeling very tired as well!

The consultant came to see him and said, 'I have some grave news for you Mr Brett. You have lung cancer and to save your good lung for you, we will have to operate to remove the diseased one as soon as possible. I have recommended to my surgeon that this will take place tomorrow morning.'

This struck Robert heavily – he had not at all realised that a 'spot on the lung' could suddenly have become full lung cancer! 'Ah well, perhaps I can get by with one lung. I'm not the world's greatest athlete and probably won't need two.' He tried to comfort himself, but realised he was crying inside.

The surgeon came round to meet him and explained the procedures to him, and said that the preparation for the operation would take place in the morning.

The operation over, he came round. He was very groggy, and the pain was quite intense in his chest. They administered morphine to him to reduce the pain level and he slumbered off into a deep sleep. They had told him that they would have to keep him in for some time under observation to ascertain his recovery. His father looked in on him and so did Father Ignatius, but he was not really strong enough to receive visitors properly. He kept drifting off into deep sleep and was certainly not good company at the moment!

He was taken for further x-rays and the prognosis was not good. The cancer was well established in his other lung and there was no point in further operations. It would not do any good and it would only be a matter of time. His father was informed of the seriousness of the situation, and he let the rest of their remaining relatives know about it. His father was most upset about the terrible situation his son was in and found it hard to cope with the thoughts of the final outcome.

Robert was now in a coma aided from time to time with the help of oxygen, but mainly he was asleep. One day Robert awoke from his coma, looked to the right and saw Father Ignatius in the room, just putting away his accoutrements for the last anointing of the sick. He turned his gaze to the centre of the room and saw his father. He turned his gaze to the left-hand side of the room – he saw the face of Juliet smiling down at him, and she was holding his hand. He looked over her right shoulder and saw the clock on the wall. It was exactly 9 a.m.

'Just in time to catch the Cornish Riviera Express from Paddington,' he said, and then he passed peacefully away.

Printed in the United Kingdom
by Lightning Source UK Ltd.
120757UK00001B/129